Rommel's Game

Victory at El Alamein

&

Towards the Caucasus

Chapters

Oktoberfest

Why do they always keep the entrances open? That blinking Ferris wheel, flashing and shimmering through the open tent flat, has always annoyed me. The shining turns make me feel giddy even from a distance. Or maybe that's the beer getting to me? It's only noon and I've already rushed through four liters sitting at this mucky table surrounded by other drunk festival-goers, most of them foreigners, swaying idly to the blaring music.

Seated diagonally opposite me is another middle-aged man who keeps giving me funny looks, as if he knew me. He looks like an overweight vagrant in a barn coat, with half-long greasy black hair and sallow skin. Not a German, probably American, or God knows what. Now the idiot is gawking at me again. He has this long scar, thick and shiny, which crosses the whole of his cheek down to his chin. With the speed of lightning a memory flashes through my mind! No, it can't really be – can it? I think I know this scarred face.

Suddenly the stranger gets up, his dark eyes staring at me eerily. "It's a small world! You and I have already knocked back a few beers together."

I smile. He didn't introduce himself a second too soon. Now I knew exactly who he was. "Cliff from Tennessee, I don't believe it! You here at the October Festival?"

"Jeez, when did you get here? Come on over, now it's beer-time!"

We shake hands.

"An eternity. Joseph, right?"

"Right, the last time we met was in the Hotel Florida in Madrid."

Cliff clasped his tankard with both hands and nodded. "Indeed, 1936, in the lobby of Hotel Florida," he chuckled. "The place where all war correspondents and the crème de la crème of scum met."

"As always happens in times of crisis. The Spanish civil war. Those were the days; how could we forget them?"

"Impossible, and the pretty señoritas even less. Terrific to see you again, Joseph."

"Likewise. Tell me, do you often come to the Oktoberfest in Munich?"

"Every year, in time for the kick-off," he blurted out. "But I've never seen you here."

"I live in Berlin. This is my first time here."

"And you, a German? Shame on you!"

We both laugh, raising our glasses.

"To old friendships, Cliff."

"I completely forgot; weren't you a war correspondent, too? If you don't mind my asking...."

I took a long swig. "Sort of, I was a so-called photojournalist for the Berliner Illustrated Paper in the beginning, now I'm in early retirement."

Cliff nodded amicably. "In the Reich you can now retire as early as your mid-fifties, I'm glad for you."

"Sometimes I wouldn't mind having something to do."

"That's something I wanted to talk to you about, but first let me ask you about your former task. If I remember correctly, many war correspondents faked the news," he eyed me. "You didn't, did you?"

"Oh, that came later. I carried on working for the newspaper for many years," I told him. "Later, in World War II, I was on active service with the propaganda unit."

"Really? So that's why I never heard from you again. Where did they send you?"

"That's a long story, Cliff. 1940, propaganda-photographer in occupied Paris. Later I was attached to a propaganda unit of the air force; then with the ground troops, air defense. And you, where have you been all these years?"

"Well, I stayed on in Spain. I carried on being active, as you can see." He pointed to the scar on his face.

"You had that when we met," I interjected with a smile.

"You're right there, boy. I was one of the few who was trying to report from Franco's side." He moves closer and shows me his scar. "This thing here happened in Teruel in northern Spain after my car was hit by Communist fire. I was trying to help out the troops from a trench. Later Franco gave me a medal for it."

"Congratulations. Do you still remember our drinking sprees in Hotel Florida?" I asked him.

"You mean with the riff-raff? Of course, I do."

"A lot of riff-raff. That Hemingway has become famous in the meantime, we used to chat with him down there."

Cliff belched. "Always in the bar. Did you like him?"

"Hemingway preferred drinking with his cronies, and I was one of them."

"You know I was just another unknown correspondent, we met lots of people, you know, but Hemingway always liked to think of himself as a combatant. Tell you what, for me he was just a bogus ace."

"Probably. But he wasn't nearly as famous at that time," I said. "Anyway, I was closer to Capa and the other foreign photographers, as you might remember."

He nodded. "Capa was another loony."

"There were some famous photographers around, though. Capa, and also the German, Gerda Taro, who died at the battle of Brunete."

"And were they that special?" he asked.

"Well, Capa in particular was known for using his camera as a weapon – but most of them shrank from battle, unlike us."

Cliff made a sour, condescending face. "They were scared shitless."

"Their work wasn't that great either. Their early photographs may have been propagandistic, but as the war raged on they lost their edge, refrained from the actual fighting. Soon the horrors of the war overtook them, and their photos became less stylized. Not informative at all."

Cliff finished half of his tankard in one gulp. "So, what about you? You collaborated with the German air-force, right?"

"Our new Luftwaffe. I wish I had," I replied, laughing. "I had nothing to do with the bombings in Spain, but if I could have joined them at that time, I wouldn't have hesitated. I stayed on the ground as an independent for this Berlin paper."

"You had no connection to the Condor Legion?"

"If I had, we would never have met, Cliff. But I admired the chaps. That's why later in Germany I joined the air-force as a voluntary auxiliary correspondent. As a volunteer, I still had possibilities as a correspondent and photographer."

Cliff signaled to the waitress to bring another tankard. "In Spain, in those days, I, too, wanted both. For Franco to win, and to write my stories at the same time."

"Of course. I wanted Franco to win with all my might. Had I been there earlier, I wouldn't have hesitated for a second to join in the attacks of Guernica."

"Cheers, you old daredevil!"

"So where were you all those years, the war years in particular?"

"During the war years? Here and there. Different American newspapers, but mainly in England. In the end, I got bored there."

"And I expect rather uncomfortable because of the V3s," I added, laughing. "And after England?"

"Well, the last years in Asia. But once in Istanbul for the signing of the cease-fire between you and the Russians. And you? You were in Russia, I assume."

"North Africa," I said. "Four years, from the beginning to the bitter end."

He looked at me like a happy puppy. "That's fantastic, Joseph! Cheers."

"Cheers. Tell me, how long will you be in Munich?"

"I'd like to stay for a while. It's a clean city, really German. However, I'm planning to go to Berlin to the victory parade in November."

"Then that's where we'll meet again."

"That's what we should do, buddy. I still have quite a bit to do here in Germany. And you're the answer to my prayers."

"What are you up to?"

Cliff drew a cigar out of his jacket, flicked his lighter, and looked off in thought.

"I have no idea where to start. Maybe I'll write a book? Or rather, maybe it's more than a maybe."

"About the Spanish Civil War? Isn't that a bit dated?"

"Not about Spain. No, about Germany. The way you managed to become a world power, from your perspective?"

I took a long swig. Even though I was already slightly tipsy, my brain was still razor-sharp, at that moment I was on the same wave-length as Cliff.

"You mean seen through German eyes. Very good. Africa. You should write about Africa. That's where everything started."

Cliff leant far across the table and pointed his cigar at my eyes. "Precisely! And Rommel, I want to write about him. El Alamein, before and after, Rommel the legend."

"If I survive that long," I interjected, smiling.

"You are exactly right for the task," he pointed at me, "you can help me."

"Not so fast. I was only a war correspondent and photographer, not a real soldier."

"You won. You're the one who can make my book a reality."

I understood the man now. He was really planning to write a book about the German victory. When will Americans understand that Germany didn't win the war completely? Germany had reached an impasse with our former enemies. If you want to call that victory, then okay.

The evening festivities began to blur around me. Three tankards of beer are not excessive, but I hate walking around the fair having to find a tree to pee against every two minutes.

Cliff, however, was obviously in full swing. "Germany showed us. You war correspondents were real soldiers and your propaganda was inspired."

My old buddy was obviously getting carried away.

"Cliff, let's keep it short," I interrupted.

"Why, are you planning to write a book, too?"

"I haven't got that far. But we should exchange numbers, and maybe think of a comfortable place to meet."

"A cozy corner at the victory parade?" he asked innocently.

"You took the words right out of my mouth."

"Off to Berlin then. Do you know a good place?"

We looked at each other and almost simultaneously blurted it out. Admittedly, I was perhaps half a second quicker. "Café Kranzler." Yes, that is where we would meet again. "At the little victory parade?"

"At the big German victory parade!"

Cliff looks at the pretty waitress in a dirndl and motions for two more tankards. I quickly intervene and press fifty Reichsmark into the girl's hand. "Cliff, the beers are on me tonight. In Café Kranzler it'll be your turn."

I pat him on the back and head for the exit. Seconds later I'm outside in the cool air hailing a Mercedes taxi, even though my hotel is only three blocks away from the festival. How small the world is! That I met Cliff of all people here and now is a strange coincidence. But I won't be fooled, even for a second, that coincidences in the wrong place at the wrong time can still be dangerous in post-war Germany.

Rommel's Farewell Present

On my arrival home, I go into my comfortably furnished basement, which is my party-room, hobby-room and refuge. There, in the middle, on a large oak table, totally official and hardly touched, lies a black leather briefcase – a present from the great commander. Small oil-paintings adorn the wall, a sort of mini-exhibition of the supposedly best field marshals of the big war, my modest selection, which gives me pleasure every day. I have to smile. Why exactly these men? Von Manstein, Medel, Kesselring, even the American Chester-Nimitz, they all hang here. I had removed Rommel's picture. As a precaution. Even if a lot has changed in the last few years and the Gestapo has been abolished – or rather has a new name now – and what was formerly the total surveillance state had mellowed a bit. Therefore, could I really hang him up again? Inwardly I have to agree and nod my head. *The great general field marshal, he had won so much.* I remember Tobruk. *How did it all start again? Back then I had started a collection of war notes in my drawer.*

I rummage around in an old chest of drawers and actually find a pile of papers from the war years. Most of it has been transcribed neatly on my old Triumph typewriter. Added to that there were old rolls of film and masses of yellowed black-and-white photos.

Here I even discover an old train ticket. Stuttgart to Marseille. Unbelievably, at that time I had to, or rather I believed I had to, leave Germany at once. After my last encounter with Rommel I was scared to death! I retreated to Spain via the south of France. I shake my head and can hardly believe it myself.

My God, how long ago that all was! With hindsight, I got away with merely a black eye. Not that I was afraid of being wounded, or imprisonment, but I was lucky that I wasn't hauled in front of the People's Court. My acquaintance with Rommel would have been enough. That's why I had to flee to Spain in 1943, for fear that I would be associated with Hitler's would-be assassins who tried to blow up his plane over Byelorussia. But nothing happened. Long after the end of the war, in 1951, when the SS had been totally stripped of power, and the business of the concentration camps was completely exposed, all "resistance fighters" were exonerated by the high command of the armed forces and rehabilitated. Even potential adversaries and suspected opponents. That is, people like me.

At any rate, I now sit here comfortably in my basement, which I use more and more frequently as a bar. I'm my own best customer, with a good supply of Jägermeister and wheat beer, so typically German, and the now opened black leather suitcase of the great field marshal lies in front of me, his personal farewell gift and legacy to me. I remember his sad face when we took leave of one another. And here it lies now, his collection of personal notes and pictures. Add to that my own material, collected over four war years, all hidden in drawers and cardboard boxes – one could use it to write a dozen books, documentaries, and I don't know what. All original material, over which by now history had laid a layer of dust. At the bottom of a drawer I find a yellowed color photograph, the harbor of Tripoli. Yes, those were the days, that was the starting point. The beginning of victory – or rather a stalemate – never mind, they were magnificent and dangerous times.

I'm in the mood for Wagner. Once again, I have to smile to myself. Cliff and I have shared hobbies, drinking and cigars. I take a Havana out of its wooden box, light it, put on a record of Wagner's Lohengrin, and slide deep down into my wing-chair. My thoughts wander back into the past.

First Deployment

It must have been the beginning of February 1941. I was the first war correspondent for the up and coming North Africa operation. I remember how, in Naples, I was assigned to the old warhorses of the 5th Light Division, all battle-tried men from France. We were more or less deposited in the middle of the old part of town. We loafed around in the square like tramps waiting for the boats, which were behind schedule. I grinned to myself. In a way I had always thought that I looked more Italian than German, and on top of that my Italian was pretty good. Looking back at the interlude in Naples, I ambled along the antique colonnade arches and squares, greeted even unknown locals in the streets, but they gave me funny looks and then ignored me. No, I didn't like them. Even the ladies of the night had this peculiar tendency to completely ignore what I said.

Then it started. One of the first German ship convoys went from Naples to Tripoli, and I was part of it! The crossing with my armed comrades of the 5th Light Division went smoothly, albeit slowly. One by one we arrived in Tripoli on little boats and steamers. On 14th February the first units of the division under Major General Streich arrived in town. Most units were a mixture of armored infantry regiments, as well as reconnaissance, and artillery-and-subordinate units – all decent lads my own age. Many saw themselves as artillery-men, even though most of the units only had a handful of heavy tanks and hardly any artillery. I was the only war correspondent and photographer for miles around, which proved to be an advantage, especially when one considered the super-egos of our leaders. But why on earth had we ended up in North Africa? What were we doing there?

I open a yellowed envelope from the drawer and find a pretty good photo of a damaged Churchill tank. Apparently, the track had been damaged by a long-distance shot and ricochet.

There were probably still dozens of old slips of paper, notes and photos in my drawer. I shake my head and bury my head in my hands. Let's recap, why were we there? We Germans, in the desert of North Africa? I find notes with the heading "Operation Sunflower." It really started with the unreliable Italians. With Mussolini, that loser. After France was beaten in the Western campaign, and Tunisia belonged to Vichy-France, Mussolini's expansion goals in North Africa were pointed towards Egypt. The notes prove it. On 9th September 1940, Italy finally marched into Egypt with the 10th army. The invasion however had little success and came to a halt a mere 100 km behind the Egyptian/Libyan border, as a result of poor provisions and equipment. Until the beginning of February 1941, the allied units had occupied the Cyrenaica up to and including El Alghaila and had wiped out the 10th Italian army almost entirely. I believe that is what it looked like at that time, those were the facts; and that was also only the beginning of many things.

The cigar tastes different today, it must be nearly as old as my historical flashbacks. I discover a note in my own handwriting that answers my question regarding our former allies.

The High Command of the Wehrmacht gave instructions to commence Operation Sunflower as a reaction to Mussolini, but mainly to divert attention away from Italy's defeat. First, a blocking unit of armored forces was to be dispatched to prevent the Allies from pushing further into Libya. The first convoy of the newly created German Africa Korps under the command of Major General Erwin Rommel left Naples as early as the 8th February and reached Africa on 11th February 1941. But the landing was anything but child's play, I remember.

I look for further material about the beginning of the Africa Korps, perhaps something about Tripoli. Underneath the whole heap of paper, I discover an old film recording of the German weekly television show. March 1941. I wipe the dust off to reveal the title: "Harbor Landing." I nod to myself, because I know exactly what it contains. The landing of German troops in Tripoli, Rommel's first inspections – and more or less my debut as a war correspondent at the side of the air defenses. A very important stage in the war against the English. Everything started here; with the almighty explosion of a steamship that had been carrying cargo.

Landing in Tripoli

We had just reached the pier of Tripoli, when behind us the German freighter Leverkusen exploded. My comrades did not have permission to leave the harbor area. However, as a reporter I was an exceptional case and had no problems. A short time later I wandered through the old part of Tripoli as dusk fell.

Cobbled streets, white walls, open shops, heat, and everywhere there were muftis running around, their sideways glances semi-hostile and judging me with their black eyes. It was a huge city even back then, with low grey and white dwellings, a few antique shops on the Ville de Tripoli; and on the corners, the occasional scribes on typewriters for other muftis, or for God knows who else. All in all, the town was totally without recognizable life. For all intents and purposes, I saw no women, apart from a few old fat ones running around in their black tent-dresses. I couldn't find a teashop or a sit-down café anywhere. Casablanca had been a totally different world. Tunisia, on the other hand, was an unpleasant country. Perhaps I was arrogant, but I thought my camera was too good for this environment.

Then there was the open desert, which we could already see over the hills. Peaceful and beautiful and totally unsuitable for war. So we thought.

Not long after the arrival, all units had to gather at the airport. Suddenly, everything was strictly organized, as though any number of civilians from the whole of Europe were gathered there. Some men, who seemed more like pensioners or strange tourists, were put into ill-fitting uniforms. And then *he* actually came, the old warhorse from France, the Führer's favorite commander. His outstanding reputation was already well-founded. In World War I he had been awarded the Iron Cross Class 1 and 2; and owing to the storming of a mountain in the twelfth battle of Isonzo, he was commended with the highest decoration of the German Empire: the Pour le Mérite. His reputation as a daring warrior made him popular, outliving the phase of the Weimar Republic, and got through to Hitler, who elevated him to the commander of the Führer's escort detachment. In 1937, Rommel had written down his WWI teachings in the bestseller "Infantry attacks." It was obligatory reading for every war correspondent bar one, of course, and that was me.

I have to smile to myself again. But it's true, even then I was more of a passive, maybe even careless, reporter, photographer and hanger-on. There were curious moments during the first few months in North Africa, like the little military parade that was staged directly at the airport. It really looked funny. But Rommel was there and he nodded at us all in a friendly manner. He was smaller and slimmer in stature than I had imagined, and his cap looked too big, even for a commander. It was only later that I found out the true reason for this inspection of the troops. Tripoli was teeming with English spies – well, okay, we all knew that. But to impress the English commanders, Rommel let his soldiers parade, and his tanks roll past the grandstand in Tripoli several times. British spies were supposed to get the impression of a mighty fighting force.

But boy were we glad when our company was loaded onto trucks. Tripoli was not our world, especially because of the thieving rabble, the dishonest merchants, and the subliminal suspicion that they would sell us out to the English as soon as they had the chance. Plus, we wanted action, we wanted to prove ourselves as soldiers of the Reich.

So far, so good. Now I have arrived completely in the past. I pull another Havana out of the box and light it with my American Zippo.

In those days there were neither cigars nor lighters; the circumstances and supplies were often catastrophic. Why on earth were we there? No matter how I rack my brains, I cannot remember what the overall strategy was at the beginning. At any rate there were no official explanations as to why we Germans were compelled to fight in North Africa. Originally, we were supposed to help the beleaguered Italians by creating a block, which would prevent the English getting to Tripoli and fortifying their connections from Tunisia to Italian-Libya.

What has been going through my head all these years, is the burdensome conditions which our troops had to battle. The German armored command, and the mobile troops who were sent to Africa in 1941, were hardly equipped for war in the desert. The critical situation demanded quite a bit of talented improvisation on the part of the armed forces' planners at home. At the very least, the vehicles had to be fitted with dust-filters and sand tires. On top of that, tank trucks and additional standard containers for drinking water were needed. In a way, our entire existence down there was one big improvisation. We soon found out that in a desert war, improvisations are part of everyday life. To start with, the soldiers had to supplement their equipment from Italian army stocks, or buy clothing suitable for the tropics at local bazaars at their own expense, from pith helmet to peaked cap.

I find a note under the lid of the old film reel, which is located on the back of an old group photograph. The note's in my handwriting. I smirk while reading the army jargon, which did not fit my writing style:

"Regarding the February 26th, 1941 status reports, General von Tintelen commented on the topic of North Africa as follows: Germany was not interested in only a local defense in Tripoli, as envisioned by the Italians, but rather it was necessary to prevent the British from breaking through into Sirte, which was only possible through 'active' defense."

He was correct. In the background of the photo, other officers stand in agreement. Next to the note lies my record.

A Grubby Cinema

I read on. As a result of this conversation, Count Funck declares that in regard of this situation he does not consider that sending the planned blocking force is sufficient for averting a catastrophe. It was necessary to send a stronger force, at least one tank division, in order to lead the defense "offensively" with the goal of reconquering Cyrenaica.

Granted, we were on the defensive side from the outset in North Africa, due to the "steadfast" Italians. Later, I noted an instruction from the armed forces operation staff, which was leaked to me after the beginning of the offensive, directly from the Division Staff, which was under Rommel's control and was quasi under the table.

The letter would probably be an eye-opener for Cliff.

Rommel will be inducted on February 6th, dedicated to the guidelines, that Tripolitania must be kept in order to prevent the Brits from becoming connected to French North Africa, and containing the strong British forces in North Africa. The task would not be solved through defending the fortified camp of Tripoli. On the contrary, a defensive front must be built between the Gulf of the Great Sirte and the northern foothills of the Soda Mountains with the majority of the infantry available in Tripoli…

I have to smile again. Without our help the English would have thrown the Italians out of Libya and Tunisia, I am certain.

I sit down at my old mahogany desk and write new notes on a new notepad. Maybe for Cliff, but with all these sheets of paper, notes and photos, I might write a book myself for us Germans, because Cliff is doing this for commercial gain. I'm more interested in history and the resulting, never-ending, questions: the "what ifs."

Here I find another old photo of Tripoli, probably not far from the antique city of Carthage. I lean far back into my winged chair and close my eyes. I see the pictures as clearly as in an actual parallel world. It was also right behind Tripoli that the true adventure in Africa started for us. I can see the dust clouds clearly before me.

German motorized units, half obscured by dust, roll towards the east. It must have been half a day's travel, that is to say quite far to the east of Tripoli. Our units reached Sirte, and then by the end of February 1941, advanced to the Mugta defile. Here, not even two-and-a-half kilometers inland, lay the expanse of the salt-lake Al-Sakbh al-Kabirah – a totally impassable terrain. I accompanied the armored division, and it was not long before we, too, were stuck. Contrary to our propaganda, the desert was not always the ideal terrain for tanks. Progress was always slow, but we managed to get to Sirte. The colleagues from the weekly television show had arrived before us – surprisingly they were all beginners, and useless at camerawork. They needed effective shots, a moral leap forward, about how things were going here in Africa. To that end there were a lot of bizarre scenes. It was only the end of February, but someone suggested that it's always supposed to be hot in Africa and we should prove it on film. So off we went to capture the African sun; German soldiers wearing tropical helmets and khaki uniforms, improvising in the heat; and finally, a soldier frying an egg on the hood of a Kübelwagen. I helped my colleagues by keeping the camera angles straight – the television audience was not supposed to realize that we helped fry the egg off-screen with a gas burner. But that was part of the propaganda.

Suddenly someone touches my shoulder.

A strong female voice makes me spin around. “Are you asleep or are you drinking again?”

“My God, Helga, you startled me!”

Before me stands a powerful body, a woman in a white apron kneels down in front of me.

Her ash-blond hair has been pulled back on her head, her piercing blue eyes beam at me. “My dear Joseph, what are you doing in the basement all alone?”

I rub my eyes and gently move her hand from my shoulder. “Nothing, I’m relaxing; reading old papers, you know.”

“Would you like me to sit with you?”

“It’s all right, Helga, it’s all right.”

“Okay, my dear, I’ve finished cleaning and tidying the bedroom. If you need me I’m upstairs. I’ll stay for a while longer.”

“Very well, Helga, I’ll call you if I need you.”

She strides up the stairs. Good old Helga, my domestic help – she's been with me for over ten years already. She does everything for me. I've always stayed single, goodness knows why. Good old Helga, back then she was still working at the cinema. Not a traditional cinema, a grubby cinema, in a former cellar-bunker in Berlin. She always served me and did anything for payment, always honest and well-behaved. She satisfied me well, and over time we became friends. There came the point when she was too old to work in the cinema, so I hired her.

Then I remember – cinema bunker. That joint still exists. Wouldn't that place be just the thing for Cliff? Anonymous conversation and more. I amuse myself with my smutty thoughts and grab the bottle of Jägermeister. Today nothing matters – I allow myself a huge swig, and for a while I think of nothing. Emptiness. Tipsy, I descend into a dream bordering on the insane.

First Blood - Matildas vs 88s

The dream wasn't really a dream. Since the war, I have been plagued by flashbacks again and again. Everything is suddenly so real, as though I'm right back there. Is it the same for the other war journalists? I grab the bottle of Jägermeister off the desk and pour one more glass. Cheers to me. I'll never forget Africa. The desert was not a calm and quiet place.

I remember how the war dragged on. In March 1941, my company had its first enemy encounter, but I personally didn't experience real fighting till much later. During the siege of Tobruk and the summer battle near Sollum, I was already working in the propaganda troop's team – although never at the front. My assignment had me interviewing and photographing the rear troops. The winter of '41 dragged on with heavy, torrential rain. My deployment was sporadic, but I was part of the troop and reported about the daily hardships.

Then at the end of March, we were east of Tripoli on a dark, winter day. At first, we thought a dust-storm was approaching, or was it a thunderstorm? That's nothing unusual that time of year. But we soon heard the difference. The rumble was not thunder, but the firings of an eighty-eight somewhere behind the dark dust-clouds, which nervously and in quick succession, locked on its targets. I aimed my camera straight into the dust, barely noticing my comrades to the left and right of me, stooping low, disappearing.

The dust-cloud got darker. The roar intensified. At the moment I thought that our supplies had made it through, because there were loud shouts behind me. A bang and a hiss, then I recognized what was emerging from the dust-cloud. Just 200 meters in front of me a tank rolled towards me. For a moment I even found it exciting. No fear, just very imposing. Clearly identifiable, a strong armored British Matilda tank had fired in my direction. Another bang, and a fraction of a second later there was an explosion 50 meters behind me. "Cover!" shouted a comrade behind me. Somebody pulled me to the ground, and while falling, I hugged my most precious treasure to me – my camera. I got onto my knees and pointed the camera forwards. Indeed, there were now two Matilda-monsters facing me. Suddenly, a shattering explosion erupted behind me. Something had been hit. Shit, the monsters carried on rolling, maybe another one hundred and fifty meters. I could clearly identify the short canon, and behind it the shadows of English soldiers. We were caught unprepared, so I thought. My amused curiosity had turned into sheer panic as machine gun fire sprayed left and right. My pulse raced, another bang, but this time much nearer. In any case, I had the Matildas in my viewfinder, the monsters seemed to swerve to the right. They fired on our cargo trucks and warehouses, then swung away from me in the direction of our ammunition stores. And behind those, wasn't that where our division command post was? The dust cloud advanced upon us like a rolling inferno. I counted four, five, at least six heavy Matilda tanks, that swung about 150 meters to the right up our side, firing in stop and go. That's bad, I thought, apparently from our side there was nothing but small-bore rifle fire, the projectiles bouncing off the armor ineffectually. Where were our new tanks IV, the 5th Light had landed completely, hadn't it?

The air whistled and hissed on both sides of me, and a metallic bang had pushed my camera into my shoulder. I cried out in pain. The comrade to my right stole a glance at me and grinned, "Watch your camera doesn't batter you to death!"

Only then did I notice that the back of my camera had hit my shoulder, but at the front something was bent. In fact, a machine gun bullet had burrowed into the protective cover of my lens, without the camera the bullet would have gone straight into my throat. I shook my head, "I don't believe it!"

"Keep calm, young man", the private replied. "It's going to start now, here comes the enemy infantry."

No sooner had he said that, when everything cracked and rattled as though New Year's fireworks were exploding everywhere. We came under heavy machine gun fire. To the right and left of me they fired back. A few hundred meters away in the dust cloud, I saw the first shadows of soldiers running. Some threw themselves to the ground, it was unclear if they had been hit by bullets, or if they dove for cover.

Despite the chaos surrounding me, I was more concerned about my camera than being under fire. Maybe the lens was not destroyed, and I could just swap out my protective flap and film? Another loud crash erupted behind me. I turned to see the tractors in front of the warehouse burning, the walls already collapsed due to direct hits by the armored tank. Then more arrived. Several meters ahead of us, we heard a number of motorized vehicles roar. "We are being overrun, all men stand back," a soldier shouted, but his words were muffled by the loud pounding and roaring sounds around us. At the front, I saw two more Matilda tanks roll out directly in front of us. My thought was interrupted by a huge explosion. Glowing metal pieces flew into the sky like a volcanic eruption, and the enemy tank was wrapped in a black cloud of smoke.

"Where did that come from," I asked a soldier next to me. He was already analyzing what occurred with a pair of binoculars.

"Eighty-eight," he shouted.

A few seconds later, another tank exploded, its turret lifting off from the chassis. Another blast occurred in the background with the same sound and a bursting explosion that no tank could withstand. The soldier next to me nodded and lit a cigarette. I found my voice, "Where did the eighty-eights come from, did you see them before?"

"Nah," he answered calmly, typical for the flak guys. "Always wait until the last minute and therefore no one knows what to do."

I pulled a cigarette from my jacket. "Without them we wouldn't be sitting here smoking."

"Maybe not," my comrade shrugged, "but they have no chance with our eighty-eights anyway."

And then the explosions stopped. The dust settled on us and the smell of gunpowder carried over the burning scraps. It was a definite success. We lived another day longer.

In the evening we celebrated, which was nothing unusual. Birthday parties were plentiful, and the Italians had left wine depots in every village. We showed it to the Brits today. We lay on cots in an old hall and made pea stew in the field kitchen. We called ourselves the Africa Korps. Some of our boys smoked cannabis, pushing the sweet scent through the dilapidated hall – a century old tradition in North Africa. I admit that many of the men looked more than tipsy, or stoned, as one would say today. An older soldier somehow managed to smuggle in an accordion. The wine was treating us well and we fooled around until gradually falling asleep.

Sometime in the early morning, the field marshal appeared at our camp. I was still quite drunk and stoned, but our soldiers were proper soldiers, and soon we were on the march. We headed east. From what I heard, we were going to Benghazi.

I awake from my daydream a little disoriented in time, but my strong will activates me. I take my Pelikan ballpoint pen and sort my memories on a white sheet of paper. I try to concentrate, because only when I scribble something with a clear head will Cliff benefit from it. So now then; one thing after the other. How did the propaganda company start? Lightheaded, I start making notes.

From March onwards, we were gradually assigned to the propaganda company. Solitary individuals like me fell out of favor, and were reassigned under the direction of the ministry of propaganda to do one simple task: to portray the glorious armed forces through film and photography. Sound recordings were produced separately in Berlin. As far as I can remember, my most important task was to seek Rommel's company and film everything possible about him. My colleagues from the *Signal* even had direct instructions about that from Goebbels's ministry of propaganda.

Spring 1941 saw things on the military side advance at last, not just because of Rommel's military stratagem, but also because of our excellent fighting spirit, but above all because of our tanks. The mood was carefree; fresh tanks had arrived, including a small number of the tank IV models (a new construction; as it later turned out, the most prolifically produced tank of the armed forces), which replaced the outdated tank III that didn't stand a chance against the fat Matildas. In spite of that, the bulk of our tanks were still made up of tank III models. Gradually, we were not a light division anymore, we realized that, and it was formally declared to us that we were now a real tank division: the 21st Tank Division of the North Africa Korps.

In spite of everything, the enemy didn't sleep. The British tried to go on the offensive, but because of the withdrawal of British troops to Greece at the beginning of March 1941, British advances in the Cyrenaica near El Agheila came to a standstill. The Italian troops in Libya were reorganized and strengthened by divisions from their motherland. In the middle of March, the first tanks of the 5th Light Division arrived, on top of that the 15th Tank Division was now ordered to Africa. Two Italian divisions, including the tank division "Ariete," were put under the command of Rommel's Africa Korps. But on the whole things advanced. From March onwards the longed-for Stuka-units were available to us, and from April onwards even the ME109 fighter wing supported us, which made all the difference! At the beginning of May Rommel led the last big offensive against Tobruk, and in mid-May the most important pass of Cyrenaica, the Halfaya Pass, was in German hands. In June, the summer battle near Sollum followed, where heavy Matilda II stormed against our 88s. The biggest tank battle so far took place here, but in the end the allied Operation Battleaxe, as they called it, became a disaster for its adversaries. The fronts ground to a halt, and the African summer paralyzed friend and foe. The desert wind was merciless.

I pull myself together, enough hours in this basement. Tomorrow I would meet my old buddy again.

Reunion in the Café Kranzler

A clear, mild sunny morning. Everything in Berlin has been prepared for the victory parade, and in a few days the official opening will take place, complete with airshow. The whole town will be filled to the bursting point, but my thoughts are elsewhere. I have to be careful, since the idea of Cliff's book could have personal consequences for me – especially when it's about Rommel. Cliff is an American, but he also behaves a bit too noticeably for German tastes. There are still enough informers in Germany that we can't afford any unwanted attention.

We're going to meet in the legendary café here in the center of Berlin. The Café Kranzler. Intellectuals, bibliophiles, parvenus and former Gestapo-types meet for innocent gossip. It's one of the most well-known meeting places in Berlin. Guests come a little overdressed, more than a few officers amongst them, and many foreigners. The place is never boring.

I always come back to this historic café which first opened in 1834 at the Boulevard Unter den Linden in Berlin Center. I preferred sitting on the sun terrace, but they have this cozy smokers' room, which I thought would be best to discuss a book project – especially with a Havana cigar and a few fingers of Bourbon. In that sense Cliff and I were like-minded.

He is already sitting there, hidden in the furthest corner, busy writing notes. In front of him is a large glass of cognac.

"Cliff, old chum, we meet again."

"Joseph, you made it!"

We embrace briefly. Before I can sit, my buddy signals to the waiter for two drinks on his tab.

"Slowly, slowly, we're only just starting," I exclaimed with a hint of irony.

Cliff nods in agreement. "I'll take notes, okay?"

"Straight to the point. You're worse than us Germans!"

"Possibly. Now tell me how it all started?"

"North Africa, you mean?"

"Your career. I know you always liked being a journalist, but how did you end up in the propaganda company?"

I take a deep breath and tilt my head back. "When I think about my early career, I have to admit that I was never one of those journalists all fired up and raring to go. After Spain, I worked as a local reporter in Cologne, and in Berlin as a sports journalist, until I was sort of enrolled into the first propaganda companies in August 1939."

"Didn't you have to be a Nazi to be allowed to join?"

"Not at all. And I was never obliged to join the Party, or take part in the courses for editors, in order to be accepted into the 'List B of Editors' – that's to say, photojournalists. All I had to do was send my photos to the RDP, the Reich's Association of the German Press…that was it."

He looked surprised. "No coercion?"

"Not at first. During the first year of the war there wasn't any pressure to write. Strictly speaking, the company existed only on paper. Basically, I had a free ticket, could go on the Reich's railways without needing permission, and travel wherever I wanted. At the beginning I still sent my work to the few existing privately-run publishers. So, no pressure from anybody."

"Then when did you start producing material?"

"I had written countless manuscripts even before the Western Campaign began, but I never published them, as I knew that my thoughts wouldn't tally with the ideas of the Nazi bigwigs and the German propaganda. Yet my photos and films were popular. Later on, I had to conform. My propaganda photos were good, and to a certain degree I was revered by the Nazis, all the way up to Goebbels. But to be honest, I was more of an adventurer than a soldier or a Nazi."

"So far as I know, you were always rather apolitical."

"Even now I couldn't care less who had the political say-so: then he was called Adolf Hitler. It made no odds to me. I would have become a journalist just the same under Stalin, or even Lord Bimbambulla, simply under anybody at all; because I didn't know the meaning of politics."

"And when did you become a real military war correspondent?"

"In North Africa. I became a proper war correspondent of the armed forces and a permanent part of the military units. As such, I was even a recipient of orders. And I was good. I was praised for my photo series and my articles. The images appeared on the weekly news program and in most German newspapers. On top of that I received an award from Goebbels.

In the end I wrote, too. In the Western Desert Campaign, I quickly realized that it's impossible to capture the most dramatic moments on film.

You have to describe them with words. I actually saw myself as part of the armed forces, and later the tank division, even though, technically speaking, I was not part of the grenadiers. In spite of all the hardships that marked life in North Africa, my excitement grew, because we were the ones winning the war. We were the good ones, or so we all thought. But my enthusiasm was dealt the first blow when I myself came under fire. Several times I only survived by the skin of my teeth."

"Let's talk about Rommel. How did Rommel manage to become so famous worldwide?"

"He was already a legend before Africa. During the first World War, in 1917, at the battle of Isonzo against the Italians, he led his unit of shock troops up a mountain in the Julian Alps. He was awarded the 'Pour le Mérite.'"

"The British admired him, too, that's well known. Even Churchill praised him later as the best German general, which I find a bit over the top, what do you think?"

"You tell me! He was clever, was always able to surprise, but was he the best? I can't judge. But the British always held him in high esteem, as a soldier he was a model for friend and foe."

"Why?"

"Well, there was something like 'fair play' between the German and the British soldiers, and Rommel was, in some respects, the symbol of a chivalrous army."

"But Rommel appeared to you Germans as some sort of wonder-general, too, didn't he?"

"That was Goebbels. He built Rommel up into a legend. Rommel was created, stylized into the perfect soldier with all the essential values that are required."

"His successes attracted the attention of the British, who contributed to his myth. Any defeats inflicted by this seemingly superior adversary seemed less dramatic."

"But we know that Rommel tried to influence Hitler. He tried to convince him to make peace separately with the western allies."

"You're right about that. The way Rommel assessed the situation at the front was remarkably unsparing. Other generals preferred whitewashing many situations. But Rommel wasn't popular everywhere: he was feared by soldiers because of his strictness and ruthlessness, and he treated other officers with condescension. Critics found fault with his storming of Tobruk, which resulted in far too many casualties. And many of his fellow generals were jealous of his success."

"Were you personally in touch with him?"

"At first I had more contact with his chauffeur."

"Rommel had his own chauffeur?"

"His battle-driver, Helmut. He originated from German Southwest Africa, he knew his way around deserts. As a volunteer, he more or less let himself be shipped from one desert of the continent to another. In any case, I had the honor – or rather, the pleasure – of sharing experiences with

Helmut. He was also a photographer. In fact, he was the one who noticed me when he saw my photos of the first encounter of the tanks outside of Tripoli in the *Signal*. He wanted me to film him and Rommel together. He knew Rommel's tendency to promote himself, as well as my skills with the camera, so he tried to get us together. But strictly speaking, I had already made my name amongst experts. I was more or less a star amongst the photographers exhibiting photos for the propaganda company. Helmut knew that. In any case, we got on famously. I remember a bumpy trip in the Kübelwagen, when I sat directly behind Rommel. We were going along the edge of a minefield. Helmut knew desert sand so well that he could see where a minefield started just from the very slight sand-drifts. Helmut drove like a bat out of hell, I can tell you. He was very handy for Rommel, of course.

"And you went along to the front."

"Rommel was always where the front was. He was always ahead and everywhere; you couldn't predict where and when he would turn up. By the way, I'm still friends with Helmut. There is another story here, I'll touch on that again later."

"Let us change the subject a bit. Africa. Since when did that exist?"

"Since the beginning of 1941, in February the army troops were sent to Tripoli, that was the birth of the German Africa Korps. Hitler sent his favorite commander with troops and equipment to the out-of-the-way war zone, because the ally, Benito Mussolini, was about to lose Libya to the

British. The 'Duce' unsuccessfully chased his dream of an "Imperio Romano," and Hitler was worried about the strength of the Axis Berlin-Rome.

"And Rommel seemed to be the Man of the Hour?"

"We come back to Rommel. Of course, he was of the best commanders in the western campaign. After the trained infantryman had crossed France at top speed with his Ghost Division in 1940, Hitler ordered him to North Africa.

"And his cunning advances in Africa made Rommel rise even higher in Hitler's estimation."

"Absolutely. The Führer elevated his commander, just 50 years old, to be the youngest ever field marshal of the armed forces. It created a personality cult, which the minister of propaganda, Joseph Goebbels, knew how to orchestrate. Rommel was the most filmed general of the German Reich. Goebbels put him in the limelight in countless weekly news programs – the general liked that."

"What happened in El Alamein?"

"Cliff, that is a completely different story – to give you correct and reliable info, I'd have to go home and look at my papers."

"Let's go!"

"You want me to invite you?"

Cliff shrugged his shoulders. "Is that a problem?"

"What do you think about our sharing a bottle of real cognac, maybe something thrilling might emerge?"

"You mean, the lesson continues tomorrow?"

"That's what it looks like. We finish the round here and meet tomorrow at the Tiergarten, the big park in the middle of Berlin."

"An honest man's word is as good as his bond," the old chauvinist reiterated.

El Alamein

I'm at home in my cellar, alone again, and slightly drunk.

Tomorrow I'll meet Cliff in the Tiergarten, the immense park in the middle of Berlin. But to be able to give him a reasonably accurate picture of the situation of those days, I have to do my own research first.

I rummage in my so-called war diary, which lies quite officially on the old film rolls. The red book. Second volume, North Africa. It's a good thing that Cliff is writing a book about Rommel, so that at long last the important points are cleared up even abroad. There were plenty of heroic battles, but what was the turning point? Cliff asked me which battle or encounter would turn the war in Germany's favor? A very valid question. Our propaganda always talked of Russia and the personal successes of Hitler and Göring. No, I can state clearly, and I can remember it in full detail, where the important decision was made. The preliminary decision, the occupation of Malta, and the most important battle in North Africa. That was before El Alamein, Egypt. Because after the repulsion of the British offensive near Al Agheila, and our successes with the taking of Tobruk and near Sollum, the real success story of the North Africa Korps only started with the successful battle and the subsequent conquest of Egypt – the closing down of the Suez Canal.

But how did this go individually? The records are yellowed. In those days I noted everything in war jargon, short and heroic. Sometime during the war, we all – and I include those of us who prided ourselves on being spiritually neutral where propaganda was concerned – had distanced ourselves from facts, which were less and less of interest. We adjusted our expressions more and more to the weekly news programs' mentality and the official guidelines that came with that.

I pull out half-crumpled photos of Tobruk. It really looked just like these photographs. After the summer battle around Tobruk and Sollum, the war embedded itself in Africa. There was a long way to go to Al Alamein.

The towns around Tobruk were unsuccessfully besieged by German troops until November 1941. During this month, the British "Operation Crusader" started, which was supposed to free the embattled towns. At the beginning of this operation, British counter attacks had suffered big losses while being foiled by the resistance of the armored group, however the allied groups started another offensive in November 1941. This attack enabled the locked-in allied troops to break out of the clutches of the armored battalion. As a consequence of that, a British counter attack developed, which pushed back the German troops to their initial position on the western Cyrenaica.

It was already July, and there were big successes, but also tactical retreats behind us. The capture of Malta ensured that our supply line was more or less safe; the British had more problems in that respect. Their deliveries arrived little by little, like it did with us earlier, before Malta. But I don't want to think about Malta now, I'll discuss that with Cliff in the next few days.

Bored, I hold a scribbled note in front of my face.

After our troops succeeded to regain the initiative in the winter of 1941/42, and to refill the units of the armored forces Africa, Operation "Theseus" started at the end of May 1942. The armored forces Africa pushed through to Tobruk and could take the city. Afterwards, they pushed towards El Alamein. The battle of El Alamein, which resulted in a breakthrough to the Suez Canal, took place there in July 1942.

I have to switch off again, put my feet on the table, and light a Havana. All the old stories come back. But that's okay, because I had to digest the whole thing at some point. Tomorrow morning I'll see Cliff again. It's important to me to be well prepared, at least that's what I think in my semi-inebriated state. Today the Jägermeister feels much stronger than usual.

Crossing the Nile

Cool mornings and clear thoughts, this is how I like it the best. It's a beautiful autumn morning, the cold orange sun throws its warming rays onto the wilting leaves of the trees in the Tiergarten – the elongated park in the heart of the city. I stroll to the middle of the old pavilion, and there, next to the Fountain of Youth oil painting, my buddy Cliff sits on a bench all alone. He chews on a meat-filled milk roll, which the Americans call a *hamburger* – new custom which sloshed over to Europe from America after the war. By now there is a hamburger stall in every German town, same as how nearly every household now has a microwave or a washing machine. You have to hand it the Americans, they've changed the world more than any ideology of the Nazis, or anything that was invented in Europe over the past few centuries.

"Your hamburger looks nice," I pat the American on the shoulder.

"Good morning, Joseph. It also tastes good. You Germans can do things like that well, I must admit."

I nod. "Especially at this time of the day."

I sit down next to him on the park bench. Cliff crumbles up the rest of his hamburger bun and throws it to the pigeons. Then he digs out his notebook from his old army duffel bag. He already has the heading: El Alamein Troops, Morale and Weapons.

"You're already well prepared," I tell him. "If you like, we can get cracking. On a beautiful day like this, I'm almost in the mood for talking".

Cliff pinched his chin thoughtfully. "We aren't here to talk about the nice weather, are we?"

I shrugged my shoulder, mildly amused.

Cliff taps his notes with his biro. "El Alamein, how did that start? What was the mood like in the troop?"

"The continuation of the war up to El Alamein?"

"My report is really supposed to be a portrayal of the sequence, as well as German strategy, from the German standpoint."

"In that case I could start with all the suffering and the bloodthirsty battle scenes."

"Just tell me simply how it went on, the campaign in direction of Alexandria and the Suez Canal."

"Notebook and pencil at the ready?"

"Jawohl, mein Führer," Cliff said, jokingly.

Well, I have to dig deep into my brain. I mainly remember all the problems we had. What most people don't know is that the campaign towards Alexandria and Cairo started with enormous problems. When field marshal Rommel heard from the air force commander Africa, that the British fleet had left Alexandria, he wanted to force the decision within the next few days, no matter what happened.

At the beginning of August 1942, we, the Africa Korps, fell in to force a breakthrough to the coast. We only had the 90th division and the 21st armored division, plus the recently strengthened 15th tanks, at our disposal.

But the British had also rearmed. Bit by bit they received new tanks at the front and hundreds of new Hurricanes. The Hawker Hurricanes were a particularly bad surprise with their two 4 cm Vickers anti-tank cannons, also nicknamed 'The Flying Can Opener,' against which there was little protection or defense. With such an air force, the English general, Sir Claude Auchinleck, had the chance not only to hold up Rommel, but to push us back at least to Libya.

According to Rommel we had more than 300 tanks with two rifle regiments each, and around 60 medium anti-tank guns. Also, brigadier general Weber of the forces' artillery had 100 guns. Not an imposing amount, but the mood was high and the troops were optimistic. That optimism ran all the way through the ranks, from general to the lowest private.

"Do you remember when the tide turned?"

I shook my head. "It must have been around the beginning to the middle of August. One morning the British attacked the northern section. With the support of their enormous air force they overran the units that were there. These British counter attacks thwarted our own attack from Quaret el Abd to the east."

"So, the British managed to break through?"

"Not quite, because the British didn't get far in spite of their Hurricanes. Our deep and flat positioned 88s got nearly all of them. They were engaged in the combat, shot down, and turned off. Our tank defense was impressive. Whenever the British tried half-hearted armored attacks and then turned back halfway, the majority of their armada ended up in a gigantic, smoking rubbish tip of iron.

However, in the middle of July troops from New Zealand and India broke in, and two Italian divisions, the Trieste and Trento, got into difficulties. In spite of that, on the whole, we thwarted all attempts by our enemies to repulse us."

"Wow!"

"Yes, we did that quite well, but the loss of hardware was high. As far as I can remember we had taken over 60,000 prisoners, and we certainly put over 2,000 enemy tanks out of action. But our losses were enormous, too."

"I once read that, by the summer of 41, the Africa Korps had over 11,000 men fallen or wounded in action."

"That's about right. But the main thing was that field marshal Kesselring, who had the say over the strength of our unit, listened to Rommel. The two of them obtained important concessions from the Italian general chief of staff, Count Cavallero, by making persistent demands."

"How do you know that?"

"From Rommel's legacy, but that's another story."

"So, you met Rommel privately?"

"That, too, but carry on writing before I forget half of it again, or lose the thread."

"As you wish, Herr Obersturmbannführer," he answered, half-jokingly.

"It was like this. Only a few days after their meeting, that is between Rommel and Kesselring, saw the arrival of several hundred assault guns with 75mm howitzers, those were the so-called Semovente track guns, which for months had been standing around unused in northern Italy."

"When did this Montgomery become involved?"

"At the beginning of August, the British Lieutenant-General William Gott was shot down over the front, his successor was general Bernard Montgomery, who openly wanted to go straight into the offensive after a convoy of British ships had managed – after long last – to reach Alexandria. Rommel found that out. I also know that, to oppose the threatened offensive, he had three options. First, to detour into more favorable positions. Second, retreat. And third, to beat Montgomery to it by attacking."

"How did you know that?

"We always had first class reconnaissance. Reconnaissance had discovered only weak minefields in the southern part of the Alamein-front. During the night, German-Italian infantry were to take the positions, then the armor division was to fall in immediately and shell them."

I open my bag and pull out a note. "This note is part of Rommel's memoirs. 'In this operation,' Rommel had written, 'we mainly counted on the well-known long reaction times of the British leadership and troop. Therefore, we hoped to present the British with the fait accompli of the fully-executed operation.'"

"When did Rommel attack?"

"On 30th August. The soldiers of the armored unit Africa were taken by surprise by a special field order. I brought a long and yellowed 'departure copy.' Here, read it!"

Unit Special Order

Soldiers!

Today the unit, strengthened by new divisions, will attack.

I expect that every soldier of my unit will give his everything in these deciding days.

The Commander in Chief

Field Marshal

"Unbelievable. From everything that I hear from you, he must have been a real leader who could thrill his men. I almost believe the soldiers risked their lives more for his sake than Germany's."

"In fact, it was often so, but we were nearly all patriots."

"Joseph, I have to know everything, how did it go on?"

"In the evening the divisions set off. During the night, the tanks and vehicles came upon huge mine-barriers, which the British had buried unnoticed as obstacles. It was round about the last day in August, I think, and all divisions fought in wide-spread minefields. We couldn't advance far, but on the perimeter, where we had to turn in to go north, we finally managed to slip through. Nevertheless, the enforced change of direction was a huge disadvantage, because, as a result, we came across the highly fortified ridge, the Alam el Halfa, with the crucial height of 132. Here, at this height, unbeknownst to the German reconnaissance, the 44th Infantry Division, having just arrived from Britain, were in position. Well, it had to be taken. But the 15th and 21st Tank Divisions were well armed, and Rommel personally went to the command post and urged the divisions to hurry. On 1st September, the 15th Tank Division continued the attack. The heavy British tanks that opposed them were put out of action. A certain Major Kümmel managed to push back the enemy and take the Alam el Halfa heights! That evening, Rommel knew that the decisive success had been achieved, so long as the 15th Division and the Italian divisions could unite and disperse the two badly armored tank divisions that lay behind El Alamein. But just a day later, the better armored Axis-Divisions had a resounding success. The 15th Tank Division and the Italian Littorio Division managed to break through south of the South African Division, while a section of the 21st Tank Division, south of the Ruweisal Heights, broke through without any difficulties worth mentioning. Together, these divisions beat the weak 1st and 10th British Tank Divisions easily, their remaining tanks fled and scattered in all directions.

“Near El Hamman the German and Italian units united and pushed towards Alexandria, Rommel only left a few troop guards in front of Montgomery’s troops, who were left in tatters and cut off. The 15th Division occupied Alexandria on 5th September. The 21st Armored Division and the Italian Littorio Division reached Cairo on the same day and crossed the Nile. On 27th September, Port Suez fell without a single shot – the Suez Canal was in the hands of the Axis-powers.

“At that time, it was quite a drama, albeit not life-threatening for the British, who, with American help, ruled the Atlantic at that time, and had few problems receiving their supplies from Asia and around the Cape of Good Hope. But a short time afterwards, we had Syria to ourselves, and that’s where the majority of Rommel’s troops marched to. From there the Axis-powers, that is to say, we, threatened the south flank of the Soviet Union, a war-deciding factor for Germany, as it later turned out.”

“I once read somewhere, that Rommel partially handed over the command?”

“On Rommel’s command, brigadier general von Vaerst had by now taken over at the helm of the Africa Korps. He was an expert and a daredevil, who didn’t lag behind Rommel where daring and wiliness were concerned. But Rommel was the field marshal and dictated the direction, and the direction was the Suez Canal and further on to Syria.”

“But at that time, the end of 1942, did it make sense for the Germans to concentrate all their power on El Alamein? I mean, you already had the Anglo-Saxon troops, who had landed in Morocco and Algiers, in your back."

"It made perfect sense to concentrate our forces just to the east of the African front. Contrary to the current opinion, the American and British forces that landed in north-west Africa were not decisive, because firstly, our provisions were secured because of the capture of Malta. And even more importantly, these troops – especially those of the British – were absent from Egypt, which made the breakthrough and the march through to the Suez Canal easier. The new British and American forces in Morocco and Algiers were too far away from Rommel's front in Egypt to have any effect there. Our forces in Egypt were also the same troops that afterwards advanced from Syria to the Caucasus, more or less the Russian's soft underbelly."

"Malta, tell me more about it. And Syria, the Caucasus…."

I have to laugh out loud. "I'll give you the details at our next meeting, one thing after another, okay, buddy?"

Cliff seems slightly put out. "Okay. But what do you think the strategy was in Africa? Where was all of it supposed to lead?"

"I have to go back a long way. I only realized it later, but the German leadership wasn't stupid. Already in 1941, they planned the 'Caucasus Pincer Movement." The objective was the Suez Canal and consequently the oil supply, but at the same time to open another front against the Soviet Union to the south of the Caucasus. As support for Operation Blue. As I found out, the Africa Korps was supposed to be supported by troops from Iraq, which in the meantime, under Prime Minister Rashid Ali al-Gailani, seemed to be on Germany's side. As it transpired, we didn't need this uncertain ally, we succeeded on our own with the help of the parachute troops, who arrived in Syria even before us."

"But the British knew of these plans, didn't they?"

"Sure. The British Middle East Commando in Cairo, already briefed by their Ultra-intercepts, expected an attack on Agedabia by the Africa Korps and withdrew their troops back there. The first serious battles with Rommel's troops occurred at the beginning of April near Marsa el-Brega. This advance was not approved by Rommel's nominal superior in Libya, the Italian commander Italo Gariboldi. The Africa Korps however continued their advance, and a week later reached the fortress Tobruk, where several Australian divisions were enclosed. A little while later they made Sollum in Egypt. Subsequently, heavy fighting developed around Tobruk, because British troops wanted to relieve the town and its defenders. In November 1941, Tobruk was unsuccessfully besieged."

Cliff nods and strokes his chin. "Okay, El Alamein. After that it still continued, in the direction of Syria. Tell me again, what was happening in Iraq?"

"During the national revolt in Iraq we nearly missed the boat. First the Iraqi revolt failed as a result of lacking support from Berlin and Rom, then French-Syria fell into the hands of the Allies."

"My goodness!"

"But at that time Göring hadn't yet turned into a perfumed Nero."

Cliff giggled. "I thought we had to speak carefully."

"Yes, except when it's about the Fat One. He lost his good name anyway when his corruption became common knowledge. But in any case, we managed to bring Syria under control in the end. Three parachute regiments cleared the situation even before we arrived from Egypt."

"Okay, I've had enough for today. I feel like a long walk. Then I'll try to find out what cultural exhibitions the town has to offer."

"Everything is shut today, I'm afraid. Preparations for tomorrow's Great Victory Parade!"

"Really? There'll really be soldiers and marching bands everywhere?"

I shrug my shoulders. "We'll see. Tomorrow in front of Café Kranzler again?"

Cliff rises, nods and give me a strange, dark look. His index finger mimes the pulling of a trigger. "Auf Wiedersehen," he says.

Victory Parade

I really don't feel like celebrating, because it never was my victory. Even so this is an important day, but not because of the victory parade.

Another meeting with Cliff. Yesterday he seemed strange to me, tense, almost fanatical about his idea for the book. In any case, I'll meet him in front of Café Kranzler.

I already see him from afar with his blue-checked lumberjacket. Today he seems to be in a good mood. We greet each other with a strong shoulder embrace like they do in the Mediterranean. A marching band passes by, playing at full volume, so we have to almost shout to hear one another.

"We meet again. How do you like the victory parade so far?"

"Fantastic, I hadn't expected the brownshirts to have such good taste."

He was right.

This victory parade, even though, technically, it was not a complete victory, outshone the parade of 1940 to an unimagined extent. Here in the 'Unter den Linden' boulevard, all houses and balconies are decorated with huge floral wreaths. Gigantic war flags and also the newer German flags, at least fifteen meters long, hang from roof pinnacles, often almost touching the ground. But there is no comparison to the overwhelming Nazi-and-flower decorations around the Brandenburg Gate and the Potsdam Square, there isn't a lamppost or tree left without an enormous flag and bunting. Once an hour the air force sends bomber-and-airplane formations flying across town; black, white and red stripes crisscross the sky like a forbidden modern art painting. Marching bands and military bands have been massed together from all over the Reich. Almost all of the musicians are uniformed drummers and trumpeters. An ear-splitting racket.

"Cliff, shall we wait for the next air fleet? We'll probably get to see the new second generation intercontinental bomber ME400."

"You mean, then I can mentally prepare, in case I see it flying over New York in the near future."

I laugh out loud. "Oh, you wouldn't even get to see it with the new nuclear bombs."

He nods. "But surely, where the bombs are concerned, it's mutual."

"Hey look," I point to a group of young women marching by, "the Fräuleins from the Alliance of German Girls!"

"Indeed, the AGG. Wow, they look even better than in films, all their hair tied back…"

"…and the close-fitting white shirts and tight skirts."

Cliff wolf-whistles.

"Here in Germany it's more acceptable to wave," I warn him.

The first column of soldiers appears down the street and Cliff takes notice. "A good goose-step. Is it possible that they all look so obedient?"

"True, not at all like 1940."

"The mood is different. Respect, but no real joy."

"Possibly; but let's wait for the planes."

"That could take a while. The gents to the left and right of us are giving us funny looks, aren't they?"

"Let's just go and sit in the café and order something substantial, okay?"

We enter the café and find a table against the wall. Outside, the festivities are in full swing, but the muffled noise barely makes its way inside.

"Nice and quiet in here," I remark.

"So, do you think the people are as fired up as in 1940?"

"Good question. The presentation and the decorations are much mightier this time. But I'd say there was more genuine enthusiasm before. You probably noticed that a lot of this is artificially staged."

"Why staged?"

"There's a lot of respect to go around, but not everybody is happy. After all, we've been living under a dictatorship since 1933."

Cliff nodded in agreement. "I follow you. Especially when you consider that a large part of the population is made up of informants."

"Correct. Unlike Americans, Germans don't have anything like the First and Second Amendments to the Constitution."

"That way of life might get you down over time, I see that."

I feel grim. "The political mood isn't brilliant either."

Cliff nods sheepishly. "We live in a sort of cold war and all the great powers are by now nuclear powers…."

I look around. Indeed, standing at the bar is the same man I had seen and suspected before. The security service doesn't have days off.

"Let's order and talk quietly. After all, we're here because of your book."

"Shall I smile a little from time to time?"

"So that we don't stand out so? Good idea. We'll clap from time to time when another parade marches past outside."

"Where do we start?"

"With the drinks, as usual," I interject roguishly.

Cliff orders himself a bourbon as usual, I treat myself to a full glass of Jägermeister on the rocks.

"Has the SS been completely abolished, or are they still marching outside?"

"All in the past, they abolished themselves," I answer, slightly irritated.

"Hmm, your photos were in *Signal*, but did you ever manage to be employed by them?"

"I got close. But for that I would have had to work for the SS. From an ideological point of view, we were too far apart. The air force was enough for me, when I flew a few times at the start. *Signal* was the counterpart of the American 'Life,' so far as presentation was concerned."

"Was it difficult when you started filming from planes?"

I nodded. "The photojournalist's job in air warfare meant that the height and the speed demanded extremely short shutter-speeds, that and the confined space in the cockpit prohibited the use of tele-lenses. On top of that, we 'war correspondents,' had to take over as aerial gunners. That meant the possibilities to take photos were severely limited."

"Did you fly over Britain?"

I had to suppress an unpleasant smile. "Britain. I would probably not sit here in that case. The Me 110 hardly had a chance against the Spitfires. When the Me had to engage with one of those, there were often war correspondents inside. Most of them still lie at the bottom of the Channel. I was over France, which was better."

"You made your name there?"

"You can say that again. Even at that time I received a sort of eulogy from the ministry of propaganda. That was quite a big deal."

"But then you became a landlubber."

"At first, I belonged to the anti-aircraft defense, and even though I had filmed from planes before, in Africa I was part of the ground crew. By the way, most of the soldiers of the Africa Korps came from the southwest of Germany, we were more or less transported there together. Apart from that, there were hardly any possibilities for reporters to join flights. That was very rare. And like I said, during the whole of the Africa campaign we were always short of planes and aerial support. It surprises me sometimes, that we managed so well."

"But in the end, you accompanied the ground forces?"

"And sometimes the anti-aircraft defense, too."

"Have you got any photos or recordings of that?"

I pull out an old leather-bound album with loose pages. "Here. You can peruse that at home. My personal recordings when I accompanied a Flak unit."

"Did you manage to shoot down Hurricanes?"

I shake my head. "We were more concerned with tanks. The famous 88, originally an anti-aircraft gun, proved itself to be an excellent anti-tank weapon. Read this and make something out of it."

"That din out there is enough to make you ill," Cliff interjected testily. "Can I ask you something tricky?"

I quickly glance around the hall. "Better be quick, before we attract even more attention."

"The propaganda troop to which you belonged…who was the chief? Wasn't that Goebbels?"

"Correct, Dr. Goebbels, with whom I share a Christian name."

"And did he ever visit you, or did you ever have direct contact with him?"

"I'll tell you a secret. He invited me."

"Never!"

"He did, but perhaps we can chat about that another time. I can feel the Jägermeister taking over. I would prefer to booze on my own. Alcohol lets me lose my concentration, which is not a bad thing."

Invitation to Dr. Goebbels

"Cliff, can we carry on chatting tomorrow – I've had enough of this whole circus around us?"

Cliff's eyes are bloodshot. The bourbon and the old stories are affecting him, too. He waves his ballpoint pen around. "We should do, yes, but just one more thing. What was this with Goebbels, you met him in person. Where, North Africa?"

I take a deep breath. "Yes, but not anywhere on the battlefield. It was here in Berlin at a presentation with other award-winning war correspondents."

"Sort of the annual meeting of the propaganda troops in the ministry, I assume."

"Sort of; look, after our victory at Tobruk it wasn't just Rommel who was world famous, my films were, too. One evening an adjutant came into our tent telling me I had to go to the commandant's headquarters, there was a telegram for me."

"From Goebbels?"

"Oh yes, a telegram straight from the propaganda ministry; I had 48 hours to get me and my equipment to Berlin. The occasion was the première of some operetta by Eduard Künneke. Normally Goebbels was the certified Wonder-Nazi, but in connection with the sleazy world of pimps and disreputable women, he was more tolerant than God. We met in the box at the opera house in Berlin, the welcome was cordial and sincere, a really polite person, as I remember it. We hardly spoke, the minister was absorbed by the première, and I was only there as a sort of decoration."

"The Führer was also said to be very polite and nice," Cliff interjected.

"Only when he wasn't the Führer," I nodded, smiling.

"Anyway, the next morning I had an official appointment at the Reich's ministry for propaganda."

Cliff waves the waiter over to us, and without asking orders another round. Now I have to stay the course.

"So," Cliff grins at me. "Now tell me, did you talk more with him, a private audience?"

"Like I said, I had the appointment, which means I had to go there. The first real meeting with him was indeed in this spooky ministry."

"A real Nazi crypt?"

"Complete with torches and mysterious Germanic ornaments on the walls. But in any case, the Doctor greeted me very nicely. He didn't look like the devil either, more like a professor, an intellectual. Goebbels was jovial, but nonetheless came straight to the point. He said, 'Your films are excellent. I don't have any doubts about your convictions, my dear fellow.

"I replied something like 'It's about Germany, the world needs to see and understand our magnificence,' or some such nonsense. In any case, the good Doctor got straight back to the point, he told me what he wanted from me and I nearly fainted!"

"What did the old malicious agitator want?"

"Shh…not so loud. Be cautious, the secret service is behind us and there are undercover policemen standing at the bar."

"Are you sure of that?"

"I know them well," I whisper to him. And suddenly I was certain. Behind us and slightly to one side an elderly man was seated on his own with a glass of brandy, a sports paper in front of him. He was sitting at such an angle that it was impossible for him to read the paper. On the right, at the bar, stood two young men who gave us nasty looks. "Any second now we could be asked to show our IDs, Cliff."

"Here? At the victory parade? I don't care – now, what did he propose to you?"

My voice is just a fraction louder than a whisper. "That I would, with Riefenstahl, prepare a preview of the next victory parade, the victories of all the campaigns up to the autumn of 1940."

"Ah well, for propaganda, I expect the same sort of slimy rubbish as the films of the successful France campaign in the summer of 1940?"

"Not so loud, please." I nod and glance behind me nervously. "Worse, with more pomp, and all tied together with Wagner's overture. But you're right, Goebbels wanted to keep the morale high in the country, because the air battle over England wasn't decided in our favor."

"Okay, but back to your parade. So, you were supposed to just do the filming?"

"I was supposed to be Leni Riefenstahl's assistant."

"Why did they try to pair you off with her?"

I have to suppress a loud laugh. "Well, luckily I wasn't expected to hop into bed with her. But she wasn't reliable, technically or politically."

"But Goebbels had so many stars, especially at that time. Why you exactly?"

"I think he saw in me something like reliable talent, and maybe also loyalty. In reality Speer could have overseen all of it, but he was physically and mentally too distant from real stagecraft. Above all, he was indispensable as supervisor without office and Hitler's buddy.

"You mean a pen-pusher?"

"The same lack of imagination."

"And the Doctor is a nice man?"

"Cliff, we have to keep our voices down. What I'm about to tell you is amazing. Well, the reception was honest, but what nobody knows is that he also possesses technical knowhow and he has an eye for the essentials. He went on to say, and I am more or less quoting, 'Now tell me, Meyer, can we use your films as victory propaganda as they are? And then I'd like to hear from you, how do you see the situation in Africa?'

"I told him my films could be handed over to the weekly TV news program without any editing at all. And where Africa was concerned, the biggest problem was supply, the lack of air support, and ani-aircraft defense. His answer surprised me. 'You should tell that to the Führer!'"

Cliff almost jumps up in excitement, I just about manage to hold him back with a quick movement of my hand.

"What? Goebbels wanted to introduce you to the Führer?! His friend?"

Smiling, I shake my head. "That's roughly what he said, but it never came to that. We continued talking about the air force, but suddenly he started railing that Göring was a loser; the air force should have supported us ages ago, then Rommel would have got to the Suez Canal much earlier. But since France, the Reichsmarschall was a good-for-nothing, he didn't move anymore, etcetera."

"Was he allowed to talk like that about the Reichsmarschall then?"

"Probably the only one in the Reich, because, as you rightly noticed, he was a real friend of the Führer, together with Speer."

"So, a personal association with one of the most important men in the Reich must have been an advantage for you, wasn't it?"

"Not just for my career. I think my words were actually passed on, because as from April, Rommel actually had enough personnel to push through to Egypt."

"The conquest of Malta must have played a part in that though."

“Of course, but that’s another story, we’ll talk about that, too.”

“Did you have the extra parade?”

“After more and more postponements, it was called off personally by the Führer at the end of '41, because it didn’t look good in front of Moscow. This kind of diversion would have been too obvious.”

“I understand. And that was it? A short interview with Goebbels and straight back home?”

“Not at all. First, surprisingly, I received an Honor Roll Clasp from Goebbels – a decoration like the Iron Cross. And, wait for it: He told me that he would host a dinner in his private residence at the Bogensee that weekend. I was cordially invited.”

“No, really? With Goebbels’s family? When exactly was that?”

“In the autumn of 1940. Goebbels invited a large group from the world of films to his house at the Bogensee one Sunday evening. It was a rather nondescript house in the middle of the woods, which opened onto a lake. The whole house was surrounded by a wire fence. SS Guards stood at the entrance and patrolled the grounds.

“Right from the start it was like a family get-together, as though we had known each other for ages. There were actors and personal favorites and people from the UFA. I recognized Heinz Rühmann, Marika Röck and Olga Tschechowa. His house was small and comfortable, but the property was enormously large. An actress asked Goebbels why he didn’t extend the house? His answer seemed revealing: ‘The land doesn’t belong to me, but to the city. For whom should I build? If something were to happen, and I’m no longer alive, should my children have to take the rap for the hatred that is aimed at me?'

"Later that evening, Goebbels was called to the telephone – some important business. He didn't return for a long time and the food threatened to get cold. We cut tiny snippets off our meat, and over the course of our waiting the food on our plates kept diminishing, until only little courtesy bites were left. Then someone said, 'Enough is enough!' so we cleared our plates.

"When Goebbels came back into the group at long last, he seemed strangely absentminded. The conversation never really got going again, and we soon took our leave. The next morning, I read in the newspaper why the minister had become so silent. Rudolf Hess, Hitler's deputy at that time, had flown to England of his own accord and had been arrested. We had, unbeknownst to ourselves, witnessed a historic moment right there in the Goebbels household."

"Interesting, but I have to interrupt now?" Cliff says, slightly nauseated. "Let's fast forward to the more recent history for a bit. I'm now talking about the victory, or rather, the armistice of 1943? Briefly, how did that go?"

I shake my head. "Long story, Cliff. We'll talk about that in detail another time. But very quickly, after gaining the oilfields in Baku and the conquest of the Caucasus from the north and south, Stalin had to act. Hitler had known for a long time that the war-aim, Germania up to the Urals, was an illusion, and he listened to Rommel and Manstein."

"Since then the Dnieper river is your eastern border."

"Yes, not a complete victory in the east, but anyhow, you know the rest."

"But we'll talk about that in detail?"

I shrug my shoulders. "I don't mind."

"I have to know more about the assassination attempt in the spring of '43. Sorry if I'm jumping around a bit."

"I don't feel good talking about such stories here," I say. The two Nazi fat cats are still staring at me.

"I'll disappear now, Cliff, I've had enough for today."

"Thank you, where will we meet again?"

"Café Kranzler is too contaminated for me. We'll meet tomorrow morning in the House of German Art. They're having an exhibition suitable for the victory celebration, we'll be more private there."

"I hope it won't be too German for me," he says ironically," but if you feel happier there."

I point my finger at him. "Be careful, till tomorrow then."

The Big German Art Exhibition

The brochure at the entrance of the exhibition hall makes me brood: 'Nordic art which expresses the strength and clarity of our European and White Heritage, brings strength and joy, and is inviolable.' The Museum of German Art has changed enormously in the past few years, from a modest exhibition of recognized Nazi-artists, it now goes in the direction of the more imposing large art, which is supposed to reflect the white origins of our people and Europe. The great German art exhibition of 1953 shows the world the elevated, unmovable art and spirit of the age of white civilization. Or that's the way the exhibitors see it. The halls are full of busts, statues and bronzes of artists Arno Breker, Joseph Thorak and Fritz Klimsch. Inordinately large paintings by Ludwig Dettmanns hang on the walls. A successful and well attended exhibition, suitable for the victory parade. It conveys to the visitor an image of a strong, contented, pure white country, which one admires and from which one can learn something. That's what the high-ups imagined.

I walk in the hall looking for Cliff, my old boozing companion and good buddy from the olden days at the newly created German art exhibition in Berlin in 1945. Now here we are in the solemn, dim, marble halls that are supposed to reflect Germania's deepest soul. But Cliff and these pieces of art go together like Faust and Fred Astaire. I find him standing in front of a huge bronze statue, *Germania Onwards* by the artist Arno Breker.

"Hi, young man," I whisper to Cliff, "Do you like it here?"

Cliff grins at me innocently. "Hey, great to see you again. Yes, it is rather surprising how you Germans always had that element of surprise on your side."

"Well okay, we have a few good artists, but all pretty good patriots."

"And the best tanks, soldiers…"

"No political statements here either, please."

"I was just down in the underground vault," he says, smiling. "The Führer's vault, next to the mausoleum. Let's go down, we can talk there."

"Good idea," I say. "Near the Führer's ghost."

Operation Herkules

We sat down on a simple bench of the museum. Cliff looks at me slightly confused. "I must ask you something important straight away," he says. "The decisive turning point for you Germans in the war in North Africa, and what came afterwards, was Malta, wasn't it?

"I'd like to say, it was rather an important stage, more or less a pre-condition for the occupation of Egypt and Syria, which in turn had the consequence that we were able to put the screws on Russia in the south."

"Good, that's exactly what my book is about. The pincer movement in the Caucasus presented Germany with decisive advantages. I'm just not sure whether your leaders planned it like that, or whether it was because of Rommel's own initiative."

"Good question, Göring probably grasped it, the Führer, although a talented strategist, was too timid and lacked the overall view to pull it off. It was more a question of individual situations that followed one another leading to the overall situation, which cost the Russians dearly."

Cliff stretches out his hand towards me, waving, as though he wants to interrupt. "That's how I understood it, too. The deciding strategy came from Rommel. I understand."

He writes notes like an industrious school boy.

"Now don't be annoyed with me, Joseph, but what I'm still missing is your development as a war correspondent. What impressed you when you starting out?"

"As you know, I started modestly. Was I interested in fame? No, I was interested in my craft and the action. A war correspondent is defined by his material and especially by his commitment. Not everyone was like that. Most of my colleagues in the propaganda units wanted to get into the air-force by any means, because that was not just the most celebrated arm of the service, but also the recordings were higher paid, *Signal* paid extra premiums when it was about bomb droppings or even filmed air battles."

"I understand," he says. "Now to the centerpiece of my future book: how did Malta start? When did you first hear of it?"

"As you probably know, the operation was called Enterprise Hercules – one of the key battles of the Great War. Field marshal Kesselring was considered the architect of this operation."

"And the Italians, did they want it too?"

"What exactly went on between Mussolini and Hitler I don't know, but the Italians more or less asked Kesselring to collaborate, because in April 1942 General of the pilots, Kurt Student, was called to Rome by a telegram from Field marshal Kesselring. It was about working out a plan to conquer Malta. The overall leadership was to be in the hands of the Italian Comando Supremo, and to be coordinated by General lieutenant Count Cavallero.

"As for the operation with the code name of "Herkules," they already had a large German-Italian armed force, and Mussolini had promised the use of the Italian fleet. The procedure of the operation was designed so that paratroopers and airborne troops would fight as a vanguard under the leadership of General Student on the island for a broad bridgehead. The majority of the troops should then follow by ship and air transport."

"Which transport planes did you have?"

A dozen giants – the six-engine large scale Me 323 – were available for the transport of tanks III and IV. In addition, there were about 100 machines of the type Go 242 and 1000 gliders."

"Was it certain that the Italians would actively support the Germans? How was the collaboration?"

"The beginning was a bit of a catastrophe. There was a lot of attitude and morale. General Crüwell had given Hitler a very negative opinion of the morale of the Italians, and thus endangered almost the entire operation. As far as I've heard, Hitler is said to have been concerned that the British would send their fleet from Alexandria and Gibraltar to Malta, and that the Italians would lose their nerve and no longer fight, as was the case in Africa."

"Understandable. What was the strategic advantage that one could achieve through taking the city?"

"Not only did the capture of the city secure supplies for the decisive battle in North Africa at El Alamein, but it also cut down almost the entire British fleet in the eastern Mediterranean. We minded the Suez Canal well. The landing itself was pretty dramatic."

"What did you see? Come on, tell me something personal."

"I almost fell apart, because the British actually let down their heavy skip artillery on the old town. I saw the sky, white, filled with parachutes. The city was swarming with militia and a handful of British troops already on the rooftops. Fortunately, the mostly obsolete Lee-Enfield rifles aimed at the soldiers flying in the sky were poorly aimed."

"Tell me more."

"There were heavy battles with machine guns in the streets. I ran with a heavy camera through the street, as a black stick grenade rolled towards me. My fellow soldiers threw grenades directly from a roof onto the street, blasting five meters from my feet. I jumped into an open doorway when a second blast hit just behind me, scrambled to my feet, and pushed my back against the wall. With my camera in tow, I zigzagged through the alley. A group of soldiers ran straight towards me with their rifles raised. One of them spotted me, looked me directly in the eyes and shouted German. Ducking, I ran to the next alley. I needed to go to the bazaar in hopes of reaching safety, but at the moment taking the airfield was more important, especially for me, because that location needed to be filmed.

"I found two German paratroopers leaning against the building. They were taking aim around the corner, machine pistols raised. I instructed the lads to go in the direction of the airport, so the three of us ran through the alleyways where once again we were slammed from above, followed by rifle shots from the opposite balcony that hit the walls around us. The youngest of the soldiers covered us by keeping the balcony shooter under heavy fire. I watched as the young soldier ran across the alley and managed to toss a grenade up onto the balcony. Seconds later a gut-wrenching recoil of fire and smoke blew through the air, followed by silence.

"We continued to run through the smoke and gunfire in pairs of three, shooting at anything that happened to move. At the bazaar in front of the airport, several large explosions shook the earth beneath us, sending shredded human parts into the sky. A black, severed hand lay on the roadside, and behind us a bloody lump slapped on to the cobblestones. The comrades were already in and were able to take the Brits, who now retreated behind the runway under heavy fire.

"The first Junker's arrived flying very low. After the drop, they made steep turns and headed back home, as we tried to cover the Tommies behind the runway to determine where our weapons fell.

"Again and again, a Junker flared up in the approach and went plummeting into the ground. I saw about half a dozen planes being shot down. Usually five to eight of the twelve or thirteen paratroopers still hurled themselves from the falling planes, the rest had no chance. On the horizon I saw a Ju flare up in the approach and crash to the ground. A Junker crash-landed on the beach and was surrounded by hundreds of snipers; the paratroopers fought back for two days until they were all dead. The most effective were obviously the British 40mm Bofors guns, which claimed hundreds of losses of those in tanks or in parachutes. There was no sign of surprise and the anti-aircraft guns shot completely undisturbed without needing destroyer protection. It turned out later that the Tommies had built a series of Flak dummy positions that were promptly destroyed by our dive bombers, while the well camouflaged real guns remained intact and did not fire on the German reconnaissance aircraft in the days before the mission.

"Towards evening we secured the runway, but there was still heavy fighting in the center, and we marched in the direction of the town once more. From time to time, solitary gunshots whistle passed us, but nothing happened. By now it's dark, and we spend the night behind the bazaar in a fish store teeming with cockroaches.

"All night, distant rumblings made their way to us, and lightning flashes lit up the sky across the sea. The British navy got to the fishing boat fleet carrying our mountain infantry men. Not a single boat made it through to us.

"At dawn we make our way to the cathedral, where British units have taken up a fortified position. There is heavy gunfire, and a few shots from 5 and 8 cm Grenade launchers. Our third launcher is still behind the old city walls, and has trouble fighting the enemy, as the distance is too short. We reposition ourselves with our launchers behind a hill, our observation post on the harbor wall, a few hundred meters from the city, and we fire on the cathedral forecourt – first with high explosive grenades, then with smoke shells to support the attacking companies.

"Reinforcement arrives from the airport, with men bringing unopened weapon containers. One of them contains an antitank rifle, and the baby-faced youth from yesterday starts using it to shoot at enemy snipers in the windows of the suburb.

"As observation becomes impossible, we follow the rifle company with a grenade launcher into town. We take our positions behind the wall of a house, while heavy gunfire goes on in the adjoining street. After our ammunition has run out, we're left with only 24 shots per launcher. Finally, the order comes in from somewhere that we are to attack as a rifle company. We leave the launcher and run in file along the walls of the houses. I'm the only one without a weapon. I feel like a traitor with just my camera. Hundreds, maybe thousands of paratroopers are lying dead in the streets. We get to the city gate, the only one on this side of the ten-meter-high city wall, and find it blocked by a barricade of cobblestones. A 3.7-inch anti-tank gun advances, shooting its way in through militia soldiers and civilians, who take part in the fight in large numbers. Some of the civilians carry military guns, some hunting rifles. At last we pass over the barricade through the gate to the other side of the cathedral. In other areas the paratroopers climb like monkeys up the sloping harbor wall, which is heavily defended.

"Battles, some even fiercer than yesterday, are still raging in the whole of the old part of town. The companies have already been totally torn apart, some mixed groups fight their way forward from house to house – mainly people from the first companies.

"My platoon sergeant fell even before the city wall, and the officer in charge of the company, which I have accompanied since then, died parachuting from a shot that went straight through his Iron Cross into his heart."

I take a deep breath. The old memories make me livid. Cliff sits like a concrete statue and looks right through me.

"My goodness," he groans.

"Shall we get out of this cave? I could do with a stiff drink, what do you think?"

Syria – We Take Their Oil

Cliff isn't in the mood for whisky today. He sits on the wooden bench, staring at a huge painting by Adolf Ziegler. He nods almost imperceptibly. "Tell me, after your victory in Egypt, did you march straight through the Palestine to Syria?"

"Yes, albeit slowly. In spite of Malta and the air support from Crete, it was still enormously difficult for the supplies to follow the moving troops. Malta was an important victory, but even so, we took till the end of September '42 to travel the 900 km from Port Suez to Damascus. And even though the British fleet was more or less locked into the eastern Mediterranean, they made our lives difficult with their heavy fire along the Syrian coast. We were almost powerless against their heavy artillery. But at some point, the 21st Tanks and large parts of the Italian corps arrived, because until then there was only one parachute regiment that occupied the city, and our infantry set out to occupy the eastern oilfields. Of course, the British special forces had set them all on fire and rendered them unusable. Even months later half of Syria was still under a blanket of black clouds from the burning oil."

"What happened to the French forces who had occupied Syria before?"

"There I have to give a big thank you to our paratroopers. One single regiment had already occupied Damascus in August, the French offered no resistance, perhaps because Göring himself had waged a telephone war beforehand against the Vichy people with his usual threats."

"He didn't mess up for once? That fat Reichsmarschall Göring, he was only known to us in the States as Eunuch Number 1 of the Reich," interjected Cliff, laughing.

"Quiet, even here there are police informers, your remarks could cost us dear."

"Why so careful? You have excellent connections with Rommel, Goebbels, and God knows who else."

"Nevertheless, always careful should be our motto."

Cliff nods thoughtfully and sticks some chewing-gum into his mouth. A disgusting habit, which the Americans made fashionable in Europe. I was against things like that. No Disney films, no chewing gum, no diversity. But what the heck, we were somehow good friends and I wanted to help him with his book.

"And then you went north into Turkey?" Cliff asks.

"That didn't happen till later. By the autumn the whole strategic position in Russia had changed."

Towards the Caucasus

"So, what do you think of the Great German Art Exhibition so far?" I ask Cliff.

"A fair amount of blood and soil, on the whole it's what one can expect. Has much changed in all these years?"

"There's a bit more debate - what was still classed as degenerate a few years ago, is permitted again - but other than that, the exhibitors have stayed true to form – especially as Alfred Rosenberg, of all people, was made a Minister for Chamber of Fine Arts."

"I have to admit, up to now I couldn't concentrate much on all the art here."

"Why not, you only have to let the whole thing influence you."

"I need to know how it went on. The advance, how did it progress towards the Caucasus?"

"With great difficulty, I can tell you."

Cliff opens his notebook again and leans forwards. "Do you have any details?"

"Well, all right, the march through Turkey, in the direction of Georgia, was the most difficult forced march of my life. In late autumn of 1942, there were no real roads. Because of torrential rain, heavy machinery like artillery and even tanks could only advance at a snail's pace. Almost every day included forced marches along almost impassable paths, and every few hours we had to cross mountain passes. The Russians knew that we were coming, there was already a front at the Georgian border before we even arrived.

"We marched incessantly, pushing out natural limits, until we reached the new frontline at the Russian border. Luckily, I wasn't amongst the first, as right from the start there were casualties.

"There were our men, two rows of German soldiers occupying a position before a stream bed. The bed rose a meter or so and was covered with vegetation. The troops there occasionally fired a round or two at the Russians to their front, whom we could not yet see. I saw our Colonel walk forward and consult with another officer. A minute later the troops on the river bed stood and trotted off to the left, leaving the way clear for us. Our good old Colonel ordered our company forward through streams and unforgiving terrain.

"I was given the order to join the pioneers, which suited me well, as I wanted to get some shots of the front again.

"Just before the village I saw a line of churned up earth. This must be the Russian front line. Already men were moving about within. Our Colonel saw it too and I heard him shout, 'Grenadiers and pioneers first! Go! Go! Hurry up!' The Russians on the other end of the field were still a bit stunned by our own barrage, so we were able to jog forward a few hundred meters. Then all hell broke loose.

"I can still recall the tac-tac-tac of those Russian machine guns and the quick crack of their rifles. Some men around me fell. I panicked a little at that, tripped and fell face first in the mud. Instinctively I got up, even as Russian bullets kicked up mud around me, splattering my face. I moved and fell over a dead comrade. As I tried to hoist myself to my feet once again, someone stepped on my arm and fell forward in front of me. He writhed on the ground in pain, but there was little I could do for him. I got up, rifle in one hand, camera in the other, and ran forward. Bullets whipped past me and smacked into the wet earth, or sickeningly, into my comrades. Everywhere I looked someone was falling forward or flying backwards. My face was wet, I could hardly use my equipment – including my camera. Somehow, we made it through, and I got my shots. When I had my stuff together I applied for home leave. I must chuckle when I think how many times that saved my ass. As I told you before, those in the Propaganda could do that, we were under the command of Goebbels."

"I was never sure if you were truly such a great hero."

"To be honest, neither am I."

"Well, from Syria straight north to the Caucasus to the Russian border, amazing!"

I rub my hands. "Into the soft underbelly…."

"Maybe I'll write two books," my friend remarked cheekily.

"New books, new brooms," I answered ironically. "Tell me, Cliff, did you know that I was in direct contact with Rommel?"

"I assumed so, you said that you were allowed to accompany him in his Kübelwagen several times."

"Before and after Al-Alamein. But afterward I was ignored."

"That have something to do with your visit to Goebbels?"

"I don't think so, because, when all is said and done, Rommel was Hitler's favorite general, and Hitler and Goebbels were good friends, which means they called each other by their Christian names. In Germany, you only do that with close friends."

"And why did Hitler like Rommel so much?"

"That was a result of his speedy successes. Apart from that, he didn't belong to the typical old guard of generals, who often looked down on Hitler. They mocked the Führer for never having attended an academy. On top of that, Rommel was unconventional, clever, and a follower of Hitler's – to a certain degree. Plus, Rommel was the most-filmed general of the Reich. Goebbels put him in the limelight in countless weekly newsreels. The general liked that."

Cliff suddenly becomes grumpy. "I'm hungry, let's go stuff our faces, and then we'll carry on chatting."

"No whisky today?"

"I want to keep a clear head," he says. "I still need information about the most important happening of the war."

"Which was what, in your opinion?" I interrupted.

"The death of the Führer, the assassination."

I nod to him. "You're absolutely right, you need to know about that, but it is not without danger."

"Still? After all these years? Is one not allowed to write about it?"

"That depends," I get up and look around me. "Do you know the little restaurant at the exit of the exhibition hall?"

Cliff shoots out of his seat as though he had been stung. The way I know him, he always gets active when there is a mention of whisky or food, probably more than is the case with his supposed book. Right at the exit of the museum we spot the so-called "Imbiss," a food stand, which consists of a kiosk with a few tables and benches. "Germans like heavy, greasy food, everything fried," I inform Cliff. "But here we are undisturbed and can enjoy German culture a bit longer."

"That little stand with the mini-benches? Funny, isn't it? What sort of food do they make there?"

"Indian."

"Pardon me?"

"It's really a specialty here in Berlin. Grilled sausage with warm ketchup and curry sauce. It's simply called 'Currywurst.'"

"Authentically Arian, then."

Cliff tries the sliced-up sausage, points his finger at it, and nods appreciatively.

"Excellent, perhaps I'll move to Germany."

"I advise you to just stick to your annual Oktoberfest."

"Right. What about the assassination?"

I look around, no person close to us, apart from the fat host, who probably understands as much English as my mother understands Thai.

"Try to simply keep what I'm going to tell you in your head."

"I'm all ears," Cliff pulls out another cigar, lights it and leans back on his bench.

"March 1943. It was on the radio, the so-called Volksempfänger, which nearly every German family owned. For weeks there had been virtually no news, the occasional reports from the front, but we heard as good as nothing from Berlin. Then the sensation. First the news flash with fanfares. The Führer was very weak, an unbelievable event."

"Only in the hospital, no assassination?"

"Exactly, we got the news and the facts in dribs and drabs, probably deliberately, that way it was supposed to appear softer, but even so, it was still surreal, because the Führer was still the boss of us all."

"You learnt the details from the newspaper?"

"Not till weeks later. First on the radio. Time seemed to stand still in Germany."

"Any details of the Führer's death?"

"The Führer has fallen, it said. Insidious traitors had poisoned him, he had succumbed to his poisoning in the hospital, which was not true, of course. But the whole world was told right from the start, that these traitors of Germany could never expect mercy. Still, we were given no details whatsoever."

"How did the Führer lose his life?"

"His plane exploded; but wait, there are still some things that you should know beforehand."

"Okay then, but did the political upheaval come straight afterwards?"

"Not right away, I only learnt much later, after the war, about all the internal power struggles. However, there is one thing that is probably connected with the whole story. Only a few weeks before the assassination I was ordered to go to Rommel."

"But you met Rommel when he was still field marshal?"

"Correct. I met him ten years ago, before the assassination: February 1943."

"And afterwards?"

"That, too. In any case, I was just on home leave when I received a phone call from Helmut, Rommel's driver. Very short and succinct: I should pack my bags and go to Rommel in southern Germany."

"He wanted to invite you?"

"Invite, order, be asked to come, who cares? I set off to the Villa Lindenhof, a beautiful mansion surrounded by forest and pristine nature.

"When I got there, I first had to take a seat in the entrance hall, without being given any information. I sat there with a fat notebook and my Leica camera in my bag. In the other corners, two bodyguards or soldiers were seated, while I waited for instructions."

"You had no idea why you were there?"

"That's what is so unbelievable. After I was frisked like a gangster for weapons, I was at last let into the field marshal's office. Big double doors opened, and a guard wearing white gloves beckoned me in. Behind an enormous writing desk, sat a man in civilian clothes. Silently, he beckoned me over. Only then did I recognize him: Rommel. He wore thick glasses and smoked a cigarette. I had never seen him smoke before. With a movement of his hand, he indicated that I should sit down facing him.

"'Please excuse me for greeting you in such an informal way,' he said.

"'I'm honored,' I replied.

"The man straightened his glasses. 'I have been informed that you still have good connections to the international press. I have more or less invited you here, so that you can obtain information as an independent spirit and a former loyal companion in North Africa. I need your help, Meyer.'"

"He always called you by your surname?"

"It's common practice in German. In any case, I answered very gravely, 'Yes, whatever you say, I shall carry it out.' He smiled then. 'You aren't a soldier anymore, stay relaxed, the free and easy way you were before. Do a few personal things for me in Russia. I need somebody, who is unconnected to the armed forces and the SS, and who will make a personal photo-reportage about the situation in Byelorussia. You travel on your own account, as a freelance war correspondent without your company on the orders of the armed forces, the legal documents are already prepared.'

"'No problem, field marshal. From which exact location do you need the recordings and in which field?'

"'Byelorussia. I'm more interested in photos behind the front. I would like to know how the Einsatzgruppen really proceed.'

"'Task forces. You want me to film them?'

"'If you can. And the civilians out where the Einsatzgruppen are doing their worst. Understand that I would pay you out of my own pocket, Meyer, and it would be something bigger, because as you certainly understand, this thing is not without danger. Not so much because of the partisans – the SS and the Einsatzgruppen are by nature curious. They don't like war correspondents either, after all, the Einsatzgruppen is behind the front. You could easily get into trouble.'

"I nod, dismayed. 'I believe in you, field marshal, and I believe we must do the right thing.'

"'It is a very responsible task, but I need material to show people what is happening there. I'm making politics, Meyer.'"

Cliff looks interested. "And you flew to Byelorussia?"

"In a special plane, together with officers of the armed forces."

"What did you film?"

"I still have the material at home, I can hardly talk about it today. Mass executions of partisans, most of them innocent civilians. Umpteen thousands. And there were camps, however I couldn't get into those. The task forces, we called them the Einsatzgruppen, behaved like savages. Men in the Einsatzgruppen didn't like to execute by shooting, even though that happened a lot, but they preferred to hang people on the nearest lamppost. Luckily, I was there only for a short time. But if you are interested, I can let you have the material. It's still classified, I believe."

Cliff nods, dismayed. "How did Rommel react when he saw the material?"

"He didn't tell me anything more about it."

"Did you meet Rommel again afterwards?"

"After my return from Byelorussia. I was so shocked that I hid bits that I hadn't sent to Rommel and locked myself in my house for several days in a total panic."

"What happened to Rommel?"

"I'm getting claustrophobic, let's go somewhere else. We're too close to the Führer, if you know what I mean."

"Your irony is unmistakable," Cliff interjected. "But one more question: What, in your opinion, was the crucial factor in Germany's victory in the last World War?"

Slightly amused, I shake my head. "You call that one question? Strictly speaking it was stalemate, there was no final German victory, but a more or less lucky stalemate, with the result that Germany is a world power today, and Europe is still white, so to speak."

"But what were the most important decisions that helped all of it to become reality?"

"There were four reasons why Germany emerged out of the situation the way it did. The successful Western Campaign is well known, and Operation Sea-lion never took place. But then Barbarossa started – the campaign against the Soviet Union. I speak of four reasons, from 1941."

"You got stuck in front of Moscow at the end of 1941."

"Right, we were snowed in, and the Russians could recover during the next year."

"Declaring war on the USA in December 1941 didn't help either."

"True, but the decision was made on Europe's southern flank, in North Africa, under field marshal Rommel."

"Which originally didn't look like victory."

"Not at all. But the first, perhaps the most important decision was to give Rommel enough forces."

"Which however were lacking in Russia."

"Not quite right," I interjected. "The really deciding factor concerning supplies for Rommel lay in the capture of the most important island in the Mediterranean."

"Malta, or Crete? I found out that it was nearly decided to capture Crete instead of Malta?"

"That would have been fatal. Crete could never have stopped British supplies and wouldn't have gained us anything for our own supplies to Libya and Egypt. But luckily, Hitler realized that at the last moment. After Greece, he had already been poised to agree to air landings on Crete."

"Who influenced him?"

"Well, Raeder was always for Malta, but Göring, and I assume, Mussolini, who didn't want German troops on Malta to protect his prestige, were for Crete. And, of course, Hitler listened to his favorite general."

"Good decision, as it turned out. But then there was El Alamein as well."

"Rommel could get enough forces together for a breakthrough, and it was one of the few battles where the air force arrived at exactly the moment when they were needed."

"Was it just a question of adjustment?"

"More a question of organization, the orderly execution of the battle without interference from above."

"Not like in Russia."

"Exactly. After the victory at El Alamein the Suez Canal belonged to us."

"But that doesn't explain the change of the whole strategic layout, and not the fantastic stalemate that was reached in Russia either."

"As I said before, the capture of the Syrian oilfields was an enormous relief."

"Right, to recap. The building of a southern flank against Russia was planned from the beginning?"

"Of course. It forced Stalin to move troops to the Turkish border, and as we found out later, the Russian's counter-offensive at Stalingrad was therefore far too weak."

Smolensk Succeeds

"Joseph, how far did Rommel have influence over Hitler?"

"Less than he thought. Rommel's prestige grew enormously because of his successes, and he often unsuccessfully tried to persuade Hitler to resign on, so that the Western Allies would be open to have peace talks."

"To be honest, that still doesn't explain the stalemate the Allies agreed to with the Germans. I always thought they would never make peace with Nazi Germany."

"Hitler died in March 1943, and Göring, as the highest-ranking officer, wouldn't allow Himmler to grab power; Göring, in spite of his corruption and addiction to morphine, started to negotiate seriously over Sweden, a settlement with Stalin began to emerge. Stalin was weakened very much in spring of '43. In the end, he was actually the one who approached Germany with an offer. He could hardly expect rapid aid from his allies."

"After that Britain didn't want to continue?"

"With Germany having stationed eighty divisions along the Atlantic coast after the settlement with Russia, the prospects for Britain weren't good."

"And Hitler was dead."

"That made the negotiations easier," I nod.

"And probably because the civilian, Speer, became Secretary of State?" Cliff scribbles illegibly in his book, I've never seen him so earnest and lost in thought before.

"Right."

"What was the story about the assassination, I mean the death of the Führer? What were the consequences?" he asked.

"That was maybe the deciding event that in the end led to the ceasefire. Because the third thing that influenced the world war decisively, and which was a big piece of luck for Germany, was the successful assassination attempt on Hitler in Smolensk. As you perhaps know, just up to 1943, there were over fifty-five attempts on Hitler's life. There was a little luck involved in this case that the detonator functioned."

Cliff grabs new note paper and stares at me as though he were seeing someone exit a flying saucer. "Tell me more about it."

"The assassination? Well, I know more details, the thing itself is still classified. Promise me, that you leave it out of your book for the time being, at least until I give you my consent."

"Whatever you say, Joseph."

"First, I got all the details of the assassination from Rommel himself."

"No! When was that?"

"Not so loud. One thing after the other. Listen. The city of Smolensk, the big intersection for the eastern front, was where all the high-ups of the military stayed. Von Manstein and all the generals were to be found there. In any case, it was March 1943, on an icy, cold, late winter's day – the day towards which colonel von Tresckow, general staff officer of the group of armies, and his adjutant, Fabian von Schlabrendorff, had worked so long.

"In the morning Hitler landed in Smolensk to meet his generals. It was to be his last day. Hitler's plane started the 700 km long return flight from there to the Wolfsschanze with a bomb on board. Many different assassination variations had been prepared. The alternative plan – Hitler's execution by a pistol-marksman – was called off because he had too many SS bodyguards. So, the bomb had to be taken on board Hitler's plane, which succeeded like an old conjurer's trick. The bomb was supposed to go off after thirty minutes to make it look like a plane crash, even though everyone knew afterwards that it was an assassination. The temperatures were rather low for the ignition, but luckily the bomb exploded. And that was that. The whole thing was kept a secret for a while, the news spoke of a poisoning attempt, and even we of the propaganda were met with silence from Goebbels. The scenario with the poison and the hospital was orchestrated by Goebbels personally, with a few close friends. And then we had the biggest state funeral of all times."

"Fascinating." Cliff lights another cigar. "And what about Rommel, did he have anything to do with the affair?"

Again, I look around me, the people walk past without taking any notice of us, luckily the surrounding tables are unoccupied.

"Okay, the whole thing was something of a drama. I was personally affected."

"I understand, but if you can talk about it…."

"I'll try. But I have to go back a bit. It was spring 1943, and I was on short home leave again…"

Cliff waves his hand up and down. "Can I interrupt? You said, you had heard the news for the first time on the radio, but did anyone contact you personally? I mean, who informed you after the assassination?"

"Good guess," I interjected with a smile. "The phone went at 5 o'clock in the morning. I thought at first something had happened, someone had died. Instead, it was my old friend Helmut again, Rommel's driver and confidant. He told me to get myself to the Lindenhof."

"And you went there straightaway?"

"I arrived at dawn. This time there were no guards, no cars, everything seemed deserted. I wondered, uncomfortably, about the emptiness as I knocked on the door. Rommel himself opened up, and I was shocked when I saw him, he seemed to have aged a decade even though our last meeting hadn't been that long before.

"My dear Meyer, it gives me great pleasure to see you again."

"I'm honored, field marshal," I replied.

"He just nodded, upset. "I thank you for the material you sent. But today there is something more important. I have asked you here for a very particular reason.' He pointed at a leather case, that lay, locked, on an oak table.

'Field marshal, I don't quite understand."

"It's all right, Meyer, please take the case with you and do with it what you want. It contains documents and photos from North Africa and Syria."

"That really pleases me enormously,' I tell him. 'May I ask, why you are giving that to me?'

"Meyer, you have good connections abroad, you are a good correspondent, and you are not a Nazi.'

"You want me to publish the material?' I asked.

"Do something with it, if you want. They are not political things, I don't have any of those, and the most important papers have already gone. But here we have a lot of my private memories, truths, material to make the world understand what happened in North Africa at that time. You know about it, Meyer, you were there."

"Yes, thank you ever so much, I will treasure it."

"Unexpectedly the field marshal stretched out his hand to me. 'Meyer, I'm sorry, but you can't stay long.'

"'Field marshal?'

"Have you heard anything regarding the assassination of the Führer? That pig had to go, I tell you that openly…'

"I was totally shocked, I didn't understand a word at that moment. Then I said something like: 'No, that isn't possible!'

"Rommel looked me straight in the eyes. 'It wasn't a poison attack, Meyer. His plane exploded over Byelorussia, but it wasn't shot down. You should know, otherwise the truth will never be known.'

"'Germany deserves better than that,' I answer in a whisper.

He nodded and looked at me sadly. "That's what it looks like, but Germany needed the change.'

"Field marshal, if you are connected to that, you must leave the Reich immediately. The Gestapo…'

"Rommel interrupted me with a movement of his hand. 'Don't worry about me, Meyer.'

"I had to take a deep breath. 'Field marshal, I shall always be on your side.'

"Rommel got up and leant over the table. 'In the beginning I still thought I could be a sort of Hindenburg for my fellow countrymen, but that has sorted itself out. Like my task here.'

"I shook my head. 'You weren't involved in the Führer's death, you can take the helm of the Reich now. The population loves you…and in other countries you are highly respected.'

"He gave me a tired smile 'The SS has announced Operation Walküre and as far as I know, grabbed power. Göring is on their side, and we soldiers of the old guard have come to the end of the road. Listen, Meyer, I thank you for your loyalty. Take the case and disappear. Do a bunk and go abroad. You're not safe. But reveal the truth one day.'

"One day?' I enquired.

"Tomorrow, or in twenty years,' he added quietly.

"I felt a never-ending sorrow well up in me. I nod at him, and we shake hands once again. That was the last time I saw Rommel."

Cliff is beside himself. "Did you stay in Germany?"

"No, otherwise I would not sit here. My free travel permit from the PK propaganda unit was still valid. The same day I rode a motorbike to the south of France and hid in the bushes that night. The next morning I crossed the Pyrenees, incognito, and made it to Spain."

Cliff shakes his head in disbelief. "What happened to Rommel after you left?"

"I was very lucky again. After I left his house, I got back onto the country road, and no more than a couple minutes later two dark limousines approached from the opposite direction. Gestapo. As it emerged later, that was the end of the great field marshal. He later had a state funeral, for officially he had died fighting at the front. But as I found out much later, it was an ordered suicide. Himmler and Göring gave him the choice to either swallow poison, or be tried at the People's Court as an accomplice. In such an ignominious way did a truly great soldier exit the stage. But, as we know now, Himmler's grip on power didn't last long. Göring, while having a sober moment, grabbed all the power of government, and a few months later there really was a ceasefire. First with Stalin, and the rest everyone knows."

"Can you tell me more? After the assassination, and the state funeral, how did it continue politically? Why not Himmler?

I shrugged my shoulders. “As known, Hitler’s successor was Göring and not Himmler.”

“He was not really a convinced Nazi, more a common criminal, or wasn’t he?”

“Right, but Hitler had always protected Göring to a certain extent, because he had been there right from the beginning, and also because he was popular with the people, and now Hitler was dead, and Göring, even though a weak drug addict, was the designated follower of Hitler’s.”

“They made peace with him?”

“Stalin was always more pragmatic than ideological, and because he had been weakened by the loss of the Caucasus, he agreed to the ceasefire indeed. However, he made an offer first. In any case, our new eastern border was now at the Dnieper.”

“Not the Urals and no Germanization of Russia.”

“Not at all, those were fantasies. Göring was the only person who had his own real power. Only he could throw the gauntlet at Himmler. The Dnieper was important, Göring was realistic about that.”

“But his power was short lived.”

“Göring was too weak for the long term, too involved with the concentration camp stories. But before all that was exposed, and the looming power struggle succeeding the assassination, he had every suspect and accessory – hundreds of innocent people – arrested and condemned at the People’s Court. Freisler made a good job of it. And yet, quite soon after the ceasefire all that muck that the SS had fomented in the war, was exposed. The armed forces themselves had instigated an enquiry, and the armed forces were in competition with the SS."

"So Göring's abdication, and the following resignation of most of the high caliber Nazis, were only a matter of time then?"

"That's it. After Hitler's death, the order collapsed more or less. Later, after the ceasefire, Himmler was arrested by Göring's troops, the SS was put out of harm's way, and the generals Guderian, von Rundstedt, von Manstein, and the civilian Speer, all had the armed forces on their side. The thing with the concentration camps, that was a crime that was far too big to be hushed up forever."

"Wouldn't the Nazis have done just that, if everything had been okay?"

"Who knows?"

"But the Western powers didn't want to make peace with Göring, did they?"

"Not at first, they just muddled on. As I said, in the end, Göring was a realist. He kept making concessions to Churchill, officially."

"But you said before that there were four reasons, that helped Germany to the stalemate, that is to say the small victory. What was the fourth one?"

"Maybe there were even five. Because the Americans were advanced in their nuclear capability, even in 1943. Ours were only ready at the end of the Forties, even though our intercontinental rockets were always far ahead of their time."

"So, the Germans had to show they were ready to negotiate because of the nuclear threat?"

"Absolutely, our information in those days had always confirmed it. We were all fully aware of the Americans' advantage, and they were still in alliance with the British."

"What convinced Britain to make concessions?"

"The completion of the new Type 21 submarines."

"Why did that take so long then?"

"That hasn't been researched enough yet. It wasn't just lack of raw materials. Admiral of the fleet Dönitz always pushed the matter, even Speer tried to accelerate it. Admiral Räder is said to have said later that Hitler himself had prevented the project."

"But could the British have relied on the Americans, I mean with regard to the nuclear bombs?"

"Probably, but Churchill couldn't be 100% sure of it. He therefore had to play for time."

"And they didn't know whether the new German rockets would give the Germans a decisive advantage?"

"Germany had the aforementioned advantage clearly visible. Especially after the ceasefire with Stalin. The British still had to expect unforeseeable surprises. For better, for worse."

"Similar to the sudden stop in front of the British Expeditionary Force 1940?"

"Maybe not quite so obviously, but different sources state that with regard to the new submarines, it was dangerous for Britain. However, there are those who say that the Führer didn't really want this type of submarine."

"Even so, the British were worried."

"Rightly so, and contrary to current opinion, it was Churchill who pulled the strings for war and peace, at least where Europe was concerned. These submarines were actually capable of severely restricting supplies from across the Atlantic, and with the technology available at the time, they were hardly detectable."

"And that was that?"

"Yes. Churchill could also persuade the Americans to play for time, and to make concessions, too. There you are, four reasons for a stalemate."

"Good, I'll have to digest that first." Cliff drinks his bourbon in one gulp. "Tell me, and please forgive my asking, but are you pleased about this German Victory? And do you believe that the world is a better place because of it?"

I take a big swig. Ice cold and pleasant. But I don't feel the alcohol reach my head. I shrug my shoulders. "Not really."

Cliff nods at me, and in a low voice he says, "Your eyes are red, you look tired."

I pause. He's right, my eyes are tired. Aging eyes with red rims, exactly as if I had hardly slept – as though I've been awake longer than others in this long life. Because in the end, the war always infiltrates my dreams.

***

Made in the USA
Middletown, DE
10 November 2018